P9-ELW-609

MIDDLE

SON

Deborah Iida

MIDDLE

SON

Algonquin Books
of Chapel Hill

1996

Published by

ALGONQUIN BOOKS OF CHAPEL HILL

Post Office Box 2225

Chapel Hill, North Carolina 27515-2225

a division of

WORKMAN PUBLISHING

708 Broadway

New York, New York 10003

This is a work of fiction. All names, characters, places, and incidents are either products of the author's imagination or are used fictitiously. No reference to any real person is intended or should be inferred.

Library of Congress Cataloging-in-Publication Data

Iida, Deborah, 1956–

    Middle son : a novel / by Deborah Iida.

        p.   cm.

    ISBN 1-56512-119-8

    1. Japanese American families—Hawaii—Fiction.   2. Japanese Americans—
Hawaii—Fiction.   3. Family—Hawaii—Fiction.   I. Title.

    PS3559.I33M53   1996

    813'.54—dc20   95-33685

                                                                                        CIP

FIRST EDITION

10 9 8 7 6 5 4 3 2 1

ACKNOWLEDGMENTS

Gina Maccoby

Shannon Ravenel

Barbara Fitzpatrick

Isaburo and Kikue Iida

John and Shannon Tullius

Sandra and Kelly Schnelle

Robert and Borghild De Villiers

THANKS, ALSO,

TO MY CHILDREN

Maya, Jenavi, Kari, Sean, Tiffany

CONTENTS

For Harold

MY MOTHER

My mother is dying. We live on different Hawaiian islands, and I fly to hers on the weekends, sometimes with my wife and children but more often alone. My mother and I have begun to talk about the past, now, more than we consider the future. Much of a parent-child relationship lives in the past. On the second day of an infant's life, the parent reminisces about the first.

As I wait in Maui's modern, open-air terminal for my baggage to be unloaded, I remember the former terminal and the old banyan tree that shaded it. The tree is gone, now, but I like to imagine that some of its roots still spread beneath the concrete that covered them.

Tourists crowd tightly around the conveyor belt as baggage begins to revolve. I stand back and wait. My suitcase and box pass three times before there is enough space to politely claim them. I get a hold of the suitcase with one hand and a twined box with the other. Of the two, the box is the more important. It holds pistachio nuts from my recent Las Vegas trip, kalua pig and cinnamon bread from Oahu fundraisers, and the pork-filled buns we call manapua that my mother likes. She can no longer swallow all these foods, but, no matter, her face brightens when she sees them.

A chauffeured van takes me and a Midwest couple to a car rental firm. They appear to be about my age, and, as we ride, I notice how differently we are dressed. They wear matching tennis shoes and flower-print clothes. I wear a T-shirt, brown shorts, and rubber slippers. The man offers his hand in greeting. We shake and exchange names.

"Fujii?" he asks, repeating my last name. "Is that Hawaiian?"

"Japanese," I say. "My grandparents came here from Japan almost hundred years ago."

His wife studies my sun-darkened skin, medium height, and large eyes. "You don't look Japanese," she says.

Her husband nods. "I would have taken you for Hawaiian."

I shrug, used to the mistake. "It's the sun," I tell them. "The sun changed us all."

We reach the car rental firm and the agent assigns me a white Nissan Sentra, the rental car of this year, the trunk that thieves seek out in a crowded parking lot because they figure it will be filled with camera equipment and traveler's checks.

Despite this rented car, I feel at home in Maui. The new roads puzzle me, and the airport seems to grow during every absence, but Haleakala and the West Maui Mountains are the same, and as yet no developer owns the ocean. The drive is easy, only minutes through town, and then I am on the road home, the road to Wainoa—the ocean glinting through the palms on my left, the mountains rising peacefully beyond the sugar cane on my right. Within ten minutes I turn onto a quiet dirt road that breaks the rows of sugar. I pass the sugar mill, a few houses, and I'm home.

My mother has anticipated my arrival and waits at her front door. As I climb the front steps, baggage in hand, I nod to her, a greeting that has devolved from the ancient bows of Japan, and she smiles.

"Come inside, Spencer. I been waiting."

I step out of my rubber slippers—the basic footwear in Hawaii and called thongs and flip-flops elsewhere—and my bare feet cross the threshold to a familiar wooden floor. My lips pass across my mother's forehead easily, and I set down the suitcase.

"How your trip was?" she asks as she follows me down the long hallway to the kitchen.

"Easy," I say. "Easy to come Maui."

"Nice you came."

"I like to come," I remind her.

I set the box on top of the wooden kitchen table. My mother

gets some scissors and cuts through the twine to see what I have brought her.

She kneels on one of the two wooden benches that run the length of the table and reaches with both hands into the box. "No need bring nothing," she says as she pulls out a loaf of bread.

"Only small," I say.

"Mrs. Sato going be happy for see pistachio nut," she says as she mentally divides these favorites among her friends.

"Make sure you tell her I came rich on this trip to Vegas."

She laughs at me, the chronic Las Vegas loser. At least once a year I board the plane for Las Vegas. I usually get out of the casinos with a few dollars left in my wallet, but who can walk past that last row of slot machines at the airport? On my return flight to Hawaii, I haven't enough money to rent movie earphones. If the movie tempts me, I read lips.

"Manapua," my mother says, pulling out the small box and opening it. "I been wanting for eat this."

"Go on," I say, "take one. I can put the kalua pig in the freezer for you."

She sits on the bench and politely bites the large oval bun. "Honolulu get the best manapua," she declares, pleasing me with her appetite and apparent health.

I stack the plastic containers of kalua pig in the freezer and look away from my mother so that she may eat in peace. The kitchen is comfortably familiar. As a little boy, I sat at the end of the hallway and watched my mother scrub away sticky grains of rice that had fallen to the floor from forks and chopsticks. When her back was to me, I reached out and with my finger drew slippery circles on the wet floor.

The kitchen table, like the family that gathered around it, is the only one this house has ever had. All four table legs sit in little plastic cups which my mother fills with water to keep ants away from her table. During childhood my brother, Taizo, and I stood at opposite ends of the table and rolled marbles down its length. After he died, I rolled the marbles knowing there was no one to catch them at the other end. They fell to the wooden floor and kept rolling.

An electric stove and microwave have replaced the old kerosene stove upon which my mother used to cook food and heat dishwater. The wick coiled round and round on each of four burners. I could see it when I stood on my toes. A turn of the knob raised the wick toward my mother's lit match.

My mother has finished her manapua and we walk together to the parlor. Not much has changed over the years in this room, either. My mother's home and her easy contentment comfort me. The old koa sofa and matching chairs have new slipcovers; she must have sewn them. Would my mother have sewn new slipcovers if she believed the doctor's explanation that her cancer cannot be fought?

I sit in the flower-patterned chair, big tropical flowers of green and brown, and compare it to the modern furniture in my

Oahu home. "Chairs never last this long nowadays," I tell my mother, while patting the wooden arms with my palms. "Every so often we gotta go buy new furniture."

"Only old, this furniture," she says as she lowers herself into the far end of the couch, "and the chair get termites so better stop pounding already. Or else," my mother says and begins to giggle, "the chair going fall apart when you stay on it."

We have begun to ease into another of our weekends. Two months ago the doctor explained to my mother—a woman from a culture that reveres cleanliness—that her liver is failing to cleanse parts of her body she cannot reach. Yet I am not certain she will die, not certain at all. Today I have seen her laugh and seen her eat.

"The furniture same like me," my mother says, perhaps sensing my hope. "From outside never look too bad, but inside everything stay falling apart."

I nod, feeling that I must. She begins each visit the same way, forcing me to confront her illness. She must understand my hope and therefore feel it her motherly duty to ease the hope away. She will not dwell on this once she is certain the hope I have gathered since our last weekend visit has begun to weaken. I am anxious to get past this beginning.

"There," she says, watching me. "Good for accept truth."

"No sense only give up."

She shakes her head. "My parents teach me for accept."

"Old style, that. Accept this, accept that."

"Maybe," she says, caught between the ideas of two generations. But that has always been my mother's predicament. Her parents spoke Japanese, and her children spoke English. My mother has told me she feels fluent in neither. I understand her confusion. I, too, am a person of two languages: the oral and the written. Pidgin, the language of my childhood, inhabits my voice, and my lifelong love of reading lives in my writing. When I must speak textbook English, my mind visualizes the written words and forwards them to my mouth.

My mother pulls her legs up onto the couch and wraps her arms around her knees. She reminds me of those ladies in old folks homes who hide in corners. Her white hair, once long and black, swinging without effort, now curls only an inch from her scalp. Old age is greedy, unsatisfied, a continual process of taking away, but I wish it could have left my mother's hair alone. At least her skin, the beautiful brown of the earth, has somehow escaped without much wear. It does not hang as if an appendage but instead stretches taut and is remarkable, actually, considering her seventy years.

My mother's hand gestures toward her left and guides my eyes to the altar directly across the room from me. "The altar going be yours," she tells me. "Pretty soon the altar going be yours."

This Buddhist altar is her dearest possession, her tribute to life and death. The altar doors are opened as wide as a reverend's arms and within them rests a picture of my father. In this picture he is a man of middle age, my age, and I wonder why my mother has chosen this picture to display. Does she look back on her married life and remember a time of greatest love? Or does she want to look at her young husband instead of the white-haired man who died on their double bed?

A little gold cup holds a miniature scoop of cooked rice and sits next to my father's picture. The cup is brass, I know that now, but as a boy it was gold to me. My mother offers rice at this altar before serving herself. Even my demanding father allowed her to make an offering of fresh rice to the altar before hurrying back to serve him the second scoop from the rice pot.

On the rare childhood occasion when we hosted overnight guests, my mother prepared their futon bedding in this room, the parlor, the room of the altar. No higher honor could be offered in our simple home.

A picture of my brother, Taizo, also sits on this altar. Over the years I have learned to sense the boundaries of his picture, managing to look on all sides of the frame without seeing Taizo. Some eyes, I have learned, are not for looking into.

"Teresa and Amber stay fine?" my mother says, referring to my daughters.

I turn from the altar. "Fine. They wanted to come."

"Why you never let them?" she asks.

"Cannot come every time," I say. "Too hard to talk when they come."

"Not that hard," my mother says. "Maybe you only want for get away from your own kids."

"Why not?" I respond. "Nothing wrong with that."

"No, nothing wrong with that," my mother agrees. "Before days I no can get away. I wrap the crib sheet around my back and you stay inside. If never did that, I no can get my work done."

"Now we call the babysitter."

"Good for you," my mother says. "I think nowadays more better."

Our conversations these days alternate moods from sentence to sentence. I do not have to think carefully about each word I speak. We both recognize the limits of my mother's life, and I am free, now, to ask a lifetime of unasked questions. As a child I was quieted, scolded for my curiosity, but now my mother will patiently listen. Our family codes are breaking down.

"You mind if we talk about Taizo?" I say.

"Can."

"Long time we never talk about him. I think about him, though, watching how Teresa and Amber play together. When they fight, the memories come even more fast. Was good to have an older brother, even if I never look good beside him."

"I never compare."

"Hard to follow a brother like that. Almost perfect, him."

"I never think he stay perfect."

"Maybe," I say, unconvinced.

"He never did give me trouble," she says, remembering. I can see she daydreams, and I wonder which day she has chosen to recall.

"Taizo was hard to understand," I tell my mother. "I still keep trying to figure him out."

"No sense," she says. "Only come sick if think about past."

"But if can figure him out, the whole past going to fall into place."

"Cannot change the past," my mother says because she knows that is exactly what I would like to do.

"How long I miss him," I say. "Who could know I would miss him this long?"

"Even me. Not going forget my oldest boy. Having you helped, but. Plenty joy you give me."

"And much sorrow," I tentatively say, watching for her reaction.

My mother's head nods slowly. "Maybe," she says and pulls her knees more tightly to her body. "Maybe get sorrow."

Though I have led my mother to these words, I am unprepared for their pain. The child knows the truth, has always known the truth, but no matter how old, he would still rather not hear it.

Our eyes pass child to mother, mother to child. "I never held it against you," she says. "I never did."

And this, of course, I also know. I feel as if I have begun to reclaim all that I was, the parts of my childhood so thoughtlessly discarded over the years. I want to go on, to fall into the past.

But my mother, who has always known me well, stands and walks from the room. "Can talk later," she says from the hallway. "Now I like for go cook."

"No need cook for me," I tell her, starting to sit up. "Can pick something up."

She does not respond and continues toward the kitchen. I sit back down. The chair feels comfortable, and I settle deeply into the cushion. If I were still a boy, I'd search for marbles in this chair. My brother would help me lift the cushion.

I want to look at Taizo's picture. We haven't much time together before our childhood home will be gone; these old plantation houses are razed after their occupants die. Many years have passed since I have dared to look at my brother, and I miss the long, definitive lines of his face. I know I need only to look across the room toward the altar and he will be there, dependable Taizo, always where he is expected to be, the little boy who never became a man. I think I can look, that I am ready for any confrontation, but I am a cowardly man and fear my brother's anger. We have a peace to settle, my brother and I, a peace a long time coming.

Despite this fear, my eyes lift across the room to the picture on the altar that I usually avoid. I'm surprised to see that Taizo doesn't look angry, not as angry as I had expected. In shame I turn from my brother, but then I look to him again, my chin angled upward in a reflex of childhood. He is only a young boy in this picture, twelve years old when he died. If Taizo is a young boy, then I am younger still. My older brother will always, always, be older than I.

My fingers want to touch my brother, one little boy's hand in another. I want to brush scuffed elbows. I want to lay one leg over his, annoying him, in our shared double bed. Those possibilities are long past. I do the best I can and walk to the altar. With two hands, ever so carefully, the way a little boy holds his father's teacup, I lift my brother's picture.

I look at Taizo, the boy who for years slept at my left elbow. But, as I have long feared, my brother will not look back at me. No matter how I position his picture—and I lift it high, angle it to the side—my brother looks past me. His eyes don't meet mine, won't meet mine, and I return his picture to my mother's altar.

Next I lift my father's picture off the altar, and he talks to me as if I'm required to listen. He speaks in no specific words; I sense instead the feeling in his voice. I do not want to hear him—not now—and I shake away his voice with a shudder, the way a tree branch throws off storm water. I quickly set his picture back on the altar.

My father wasn't happy when I married Caroline—"Why you like marry one Haole?" he demanded. I answered weakly that inside we were the same color. He shook his head at my explanation and avoided us until Teresa was born. Caroline is a kind mother, the same as my own, and only then could my father accept my Caucasian wife.

I open the little drawer beneath the altar and see that my mother still has the funeral pictures. In the funerals of my childhood, all surviving relatives stood beside the casket for a photo. The photos were long and narrow, the same as the line of relatives. We rolled them into scrolls and my mother placed them in this drawer. I cannot tell by looking at the scrolls which one is from Taizo's funeral and so I begin unrolling and rerolling until I find it.

"You not coming for eat?" I hear. My mother is coming down the hallway, and I'm not ready to talk about funerals. I let go of the photo with one hand and it rerolls. Quickly I lay Taizo's funeral picture among the others in the drawer and close it. "You no can hear, or what?" she teases from the doorway.

We sit alongside each other at the kitchen table. Dishes of miso soup, shrimp tempura, pork tofu, asparagus, and lychee are arranged on the far side of our plates. My mother has already scooped the rice into my rice bowl. "No take too much lychee," she says, as if I'm a naughty little boy who will eat only fruit for dinner. My mother does not know that I am indifferent to lychee, that I have not craved the fruit for many years. She only knows it was a childhood favorite of mine, and I can guess that she asked all around the neighborhood to get it for me.

"I'll try not to be greedy," I respond, and then I pick up the ceramic bowl and drop all the lychee—every last one of them—onto my plate.

"Oh, you," my mother scolds, "still same. Always taking my lychee."

"Before days I put them in my pockets," I say, remembering how I used to take the fruits from the kitchen counter and stuff them into my overalls.

"And you think I never know," she says. "One boy walking past with big pockets. Who not going know?"

I smile at the memory of the bare-footed boy with pockets of lychee. She had known and let me walk past anyway. "Only going eat that?" I ask, looking at her plate. She has always been a light eater, weighing less than ninety pounds, but today her plate is nearly empty.

"I ate the manapua, that's why," she says. "Maybe if you no bring me the manapua I can eat." Then her shoulders shrug, a shrug of never mind, and she adds, "I not so hungry already."

"Yes, well, no go take my lychee."

"Oh, you one for talk. When you one boy, I no can hide it. Every time can find."

"Long time, already," I say, lifting my plate and pouring the lychee back into their bowl.

"Yes, for you long time. For me not long."

I nod and with chopsticks reach for shrimp. My mother calls chopsticks by their respectful Japanese name, ohashi, and believes food tastes better with a neutral wooden utensil. In my own home we use forks much more often than chopsticks.

"William write you?" I ask.

"Sent one birthday card."

"How he's doing?"

"Okay, I guess," she says. "Get one picture of the new daughter."

"Would be good to see him."

"Why you never go Seattle then? Not that far."

"No, not far," I say.

"Only get one cousin," my mother continues. "Why you never keep closer touch?"

"That's how," I say. "What I going say? Nothing to write about."

"No need write anything. Can send one card. He sure looks like your father, but. Sometimes I no can believe."

"Even me. When I saw him that time at Auntie's funeral, he looked same like Dad. Same face, those two."

"Same-same," agrees my mother, leaning over to look inside my rice bowl. She notices I've eaten all of my rice and scoops another serving into the small, triangular bowl.

"He looks like Dad," I say, nodding to thank her for the rice, "but he acts nothing like him. William is easy to figure out. Not Dad, but. I never knew what Dad was thinking."

"Yes, that's how. From the very beginning he was same. When I came pregnant with Taizo, I never know if he going marry me or not."

"See," I tease her. "Suppose to get married first. Then you no need worry."

"I know. Some worry. I never know what my parents going say. But Hiroshi good. He came with me for tell my parents about the baby. I ever tell you Taizo was one cane field baby?"

"Taizo? One cane field baby?" I ask, trying to imagine my parents lying together between rows of cane. When Caroline had difficulty conceiving early in our marriage, the old folks said we needed a cane field and a full moon. But my mother? This is the first time I have heard about the cane field. "Back then they did that, too?" I ask.

"Yes," confirms my mother, "back then we did that too." She pours tea, beginning with my cup, and continues. "When I tell my parents, they never shame me. Instead my dad came mad with Hiroshi. 'You not the one put kiawe in the cane?' my father asked."

"Why?" I say. "Why he asked that?"

"Naughty boys did that before days. They get kiawe branches —sharp, those thorns—and hide them inside one big stack of cane."

"What, some worker would stick his hand with the kiawe branch?" I ask, dipping asparagus into mayonnaise.

"No, more worse than that. The whole mill need for shut down. Kiawe ruins the crusher machine. Cannot get parts in before days—gotta get from Oahu or the mainland—so maybe would take one week for fix. Hiroshi never like answer my father so he ask him again. 'Maybe you never hear,' he said. 'You put kiawe in the cane?' I stay scared we not going get permission to marry if he never hurry up and answer my father. Then he look straight at my father and said, 'Yes, I put kiawe inside.' My father began to yell: 'How can work when mill stay close? How can buy rice when no more money?'

"I never know what Hiroshi going answer," my mother continues. "Nothing going satisfy my father. And Hiroshi never try make excuse. I remember him pull his shoulders back—brave, him—and finally I know he not going say anymore. My father knows same thing. His head shook—he was some mad—but then he came more quiet. 'Can understand,' my father said. 'You no try give excuse.' My father's nod came more strong. 'Yes,' he said, 'no make excuse. Going make one good husband for Mariko.'"

My lips sip the green tea. "Then you got married," I say.

"Yes, get. That's when Hiroshi tell me the truth."

"The truth? What truth?"

"He never even put kiawe inside the cane. Was Uncle Toshi did it."

"Uncle Toshi? Why Daddy never told your father?"

"That's what I ask him. I no can understand because what if my father said no can get married? And Hiroshi never even did nothing. So I ask Hiroshi, and he said him the oldest brother. The oldest brother stay responsible for the younger brother."

"What for? Not children," I say.

"Age never mean nothing."

"He believed in tradition," I say. "Some seriously he took all that."

"Same like Taizo," my mother says. "Taizo was same kind of big brother."

Taizo . . . Taizo . . . Taizo . . . I lower my eyes into the green tea, the fluid bound on all sides, safe, controlled, and for only a moment I lower my head into the memory of Taizo's death. The water washes the kind brown from his eyes.

An hour later, my mother and I sit together on the front porch steps. She shivers. "Cold," she says. I feel a certain horror in her chill because it is not cold. Wanting her to be comfortable, I retrieve a sweater from her bedroom doorknob and help her to put it on.

"Feels better," she says. "You not cold?"

"No, not cold," I say.

"You like it cold."

She's right, I do like the cold, but this is not cold. I feel worried because my mother is dying and now she is cold.

"Why not come live with Caroline and me?" I ask her. I have said this many times, but I want to make sure she understands that she is welcome.

"No need worry," she tells me. "If need to, I coming. Right now no need."

"Today you look only good," I say. "Today hard to believe you feel sick."

"Some days more better than others. Today feel good."

"You been to see the doctor?"

"Yes, I go every time. Same old thing. What for even go? Might as well save my money."

"No be silly. We can always help with money. No need worry about that."

"No, not worried, but doctor never do nothing. Only says same thing every time."

"I feel better when you go," I say, and wrap my arm around my mother's sweatered shoulder. She is tiny alongside me. "It's more better for me when you go to the doctor," I tell her.

"Yes, well, why you think I go?" she replies. She lifts both hands to her shoulder where they fit easily into one of mine.

WILLIAM'S

BIRTH

The sugar plantation, controlled by a large Hawaii corporation, built and owned my childhood home behind the mill. Each cluster of homes housed a specific ethnic group and intercultural marriages were rare. We referred to these house groupings not as neighborhoods but as camps, and because the dirt roads alongside the houses weren't named, we called each line of homes by row number. My family lived in Japanese Camp, Row Three, and so, like the sugar cane that surrounded me, I grew to maturity in a row.

Ethnic groups differed at the various plantations in Hawaii, and ours included, by descending population, Japanese, Filipino, Portuguese, Chinese, Puerto Rican, and Hawaiian. None of these groups held the power in Wainoa—all the power rested with the Caucasians, people we called Haoles. The Haoles were management, and the rest of us were union, a hierarchy that would change too late to benefit my father. The Haoles lived in spacious homes past the camps in Supervisors Row and planted grass instead of vegetable gardens. On one occasion when a new boss from the mainland could not pronounce *Hiroshi*, my father's name, he assigned my father the name Howard. My mother, whose name is Mariko, became Mary. It was easier, the man decided. The names gradually became part of my parents' identities, and when my father died many years later, his obituary read: Howard Hiroshi Fujii.

Early in this century, my grandfathers worked the cane fields of Wainoa. They had planned to return to their homeland after completing a three-year contract, and I wonder how many days they hoed beneath relentless sun before realizing they could never accumulate enough money for a proud return to Japan. So they remained in Wainoa, writing to relatives in Japan for help in finding wives. Suitable young women were chosen for my grandfathers, and their photos were mailed across the Pacific. Each of the men mailed his own picture in return. With photos in hand, my grandparents met. They easily identified each other, but others who had substituted more attractive photos in place of their own wandered the docks for a long time looking for their mates.

My parents taught me to refer to these first-generation immigrants as Issei. It is almost as if their identifying characteristics—

age, preference for Japanese language, adherence to traditional customs—have blended into one man, one woman, and been given a name. The second generation, first to be born on Hawaii soil, we call the Nisei. My parents were born amidst the rows and pungent smells of sugar cane, and there my father also died.

"Some good you get away from sugar," my father told me in his later years. "Only work so hard for get you away." I nodded obediently, a grown man still acquiescing to a Nisei father.

I am of the Sansei generation. We are the dreams of our parents, dreams scarred with the thorns of cane leaves and pineapples. My own children are Yonsei, and with each generation, we lose more tradition. My daughter Teresa does not care for rice, and I find this disturbing.

Taizo and I were born during the difficult years of World War II. Hawaii residents received army gas masks, and as war babies we got the specially designed bunny masks for infants, complete with floppy ears.

Unlike the Americans of Japanese ancestry in the U.S. mainland who were systematically interned without rights, the government left most of the Hawaii sugar workers alone. Approximately one percent of Hawaii's population was interned, however, and most were grabbed from their homes the night after the Pearl Harbor bombing. Japanese-language newspapers were ordered to stop printing, and the threatening news traveled up and down the rows of cane fields. Our Buddhist reverend was interned in that huge sweep of December 7, 1941, and my parents watched from their darkened home as the FBI took him away.

"Hiroshi," my mother urgently called. She looked out the front window through a slice in the curtains. "Something wrong at reverend house."

My father hurried over beside her and parted the curtains a little farther. "What they doing?"

"Get uniform and never knock."

"Front door opening," my father said.

The reverend walked down the front steps of his home with a uniformed man on each side of him, holding his arms. A third man walked behind with a suitcase.

"Get suitcase," my mother said. "What for need suitcase?"

"He not coming back."

"He never do nothing," my mother said. "Why they take him?"

"From Japan, him."

"He not helping Japan, but," my mother said. "Not like Honolulu reverend. Somebody said he tell kids for collect silver gum wrappers. Send them Japan for make metal. Only fair they take him."

"I can go help," my father said.

"No can," warned my mother. "Only take you, too."

"Somebody need for go outside," my father said. "Who will help if they come for take me? What if the neighbors only hide behind curtain? Now Japanese Camp get one empty house. Who next?"

"Quick, close curtain already," my mother said, pulling shut the material. "The car getting ready for go. No let them see us."

"I going outside."

"No can," she pleaded, grabbing his hand.

"I going," said my father, pushing her hand away. He walked to the door and opened it. Without a glance at my mother, he crossed the porch, continued down the steps, and strode purposefully to the road. He stood at the road's edge and watched as they guided the reverend's shoulders into the back seat. Other front doors opened in Row Three. Mr. Taketa stood on his porch, and Mr. Sato walked all the way to the road opposite Dad. My mother, fearful, watched Dad's back through parted curtains as the car began heading down the road with the reverend.

She winced as Dad stepped deliberately into the road and folded his arms. He faced the car in solid stance. As the car passed him, he stared boldly inside. He wanted to see their faces and for them to see his, but he said nobody looked back at him, not even the reverend.

The next day, while my father's only brother—my Uncle Toshi—guarded the shoreline with the 299th Infantry Regiment, and Harumi Shima from Row Four neared his death as a member of what would become the 442nd Regimental Combat Team, my mother gathered the old family photos from Japan and destroyed them.

I have tried to imagine this. My mother carries Taizo in her womb. Frightened at her country's anger against her skin, her blood, the shape of her eyes, she retrieves the box of photos from the closet shelf and examines them for signs of Japan: this one to keep, this photo to throw away. Her fear intensifies and she hurries, hardly glancing at the faces of relatives now the enemy. Grandparents and others are dropped at her feet where she will gather them for the trash.

And then, unexpectedly, for she has forgotten this picture, she looks into the eyes of a picture bride. Her mother, my grandmother, smiles with the ease of a young girl, hardly a woman, a hopeful bride in a gold-threaded kimono. My mother thinks of her father standing at the harbor, waiting, holding this picture in his cane-bitten hand. This is a picture she cannot bring herself to throw away. She walks to the kitchen and above a heavy pan in her sink, she lights a corner of the picture and flames take hold. The kimono first alights, and then the skin of my grandmother. My mother feels the tug of her ancestry pulling, fighting, a plea in the spark of the fire, and then the burning picture curls onto itself. My mother bends down on her knees and curls around Taizo.

The Buddhist altar, my mother's most cherished possession, also worried her during the war years and so she hid it on her closet floor behind muumuu dresses, bringing her rice offerings to the closet and praying they wouldn't come to take her husband away.

In Wainoa the wind nearly always blows, and the morning that begins my conscious memory included the wind. My shirt thumped behind my back, and palm leaves clacked one against another. All the plants in our neighborhood slanted west, away from the wind, away from the ocean.

The war was over by now, and Uncle Toshi had returned to work in the cane fields. I was five years old and Taizo was seven as we sat alongside each other on our home's front steps. The air hung wet, as if Taizo could drink it with the straw that dangled from his mouth. We were planning the day ahead—which mango trees to climb, which direction to head—as my mother hung laundry on the porch behind us. I could feel the wind, rocking, rocking, and my brother at my side, my mother at my back. Surely I would not have remembered such a day, one like any other, if it hadn't been the day William was born.

My hips crowded against Taizo's until the marbles in our overall pockets bumped together. I purposely leaned my shoulder against his. "No need sit close," he complained. I realized he needed space between us and reluctantly scooted over. My brother and I calculated distances with a different mathematics. Whenever I tried to move close to Taizo, near enough to touch, he moved away. If he were physically unable to move away from me, like when we all crowded into my neighbor's car and drove around the mountains to Lahaina, then he mentally detached. For me that was even worse. To this day, I hate when a mind turns away from me.

The sounds of my mother were the sounds of housework: the sweeping broom, the swishing rice, the rhythmic rub of the charcoal iron. Taizo and I listened from the front steps that morning as she methodically hung laundry across the porch, her rubber slippers shuffling along the wooden floorboards. Clothespins shifted and clicked inside the cloth bag that hung from her shoulder. Ever polite, my mother hung inoffensive shirts on the clothesline in view of the neighbors and worked her way inward toward our front door and the family underwear.

Her silent slippers, the absence of sound, turned me around. Otherwise, I would not have seen the blood-tinged waters pour from her womb. My eyes followed my mother's down her housedress, her legs, and settled on her rubber slippers wet with inner waters that trickled through the porch's wooden slats.

After her waters slowed, my mother mopped the porch and packed a bag. With the cotton bag over one arm and her purse over the other, she hurried Taizo and me across one row of homes to Auntie Sachi's. She was married to my Uncle Toshi and could watch us while Mom was in the hospital. My mother then had to walk the mile past the camps to the plantation hospital. A few times when she was still within sight, she turned and waved. I waved back with both hands in the air, jumping up and down. Taizo kept his hands under control in his pockets.

William was born later that day. Although the position would be temporary, I became a middle son.

The next morning Taizo and I ran ahead of Auntie to visit Mom at the hospital. The hospital, like our home, was owned by the plantation. The four-sided, one-window-to-a-room building was basic and functional. The plantation had the knack of providing all of life's necessities and that was it. Not a window extra.

Taizo and I were too young to enter the hospital, but we were hoping to talk to Mom through an open window. We didn't know which room was hers, though. We peeked through the first window at the end of the building and saw Marc Yamada's mom hemming a pair of pants on her bed.

"Taizo . . . Spencer," she greeted from her bed. "Came for visit Mommy?"

"Yes," I said. "Taizo never know which window for check."

He stared at me and quickly whispered, "You never know, too."

"Your mom stay two windows down," said Mrs. Yamada, biting the thread between her teeth. "Some cute, the baby. Too bad you no stay old enough for come inside."

"Two windows down?" I said.

"Mr. Okamoto stay in the room between us. Never get room on the men's side so he get put with the ladies. Grumble, grumble. You know him."

I looked at Taizo and wondered if he was thinking like I was—avoid Mr. Okamoto's window.

"Go already, boys. I think your mommy stay waiting for you.

Say hi next time, but. This room stay boring. They never like let me out bed."

" 'Bye, Auntie," I said. We called any adult in Japanese Camp by the titles "Auntie" and "Uncle."

" 'Bye. No forget come back for see me."

Taizo and I hurried toward Mom. We each ducked beneath Mr. Okamoto's window without discussing it beforehand. He forbade all the neighborhood boys to climb his mango tree or take a shortcut through his yard. We had nothing to talk about.

Once past his window, we ran to Mom's. I put my hands on the windowsill and leaned inside. "Mommy," I said. "Hi, Mom."

She sat up in bed and turned to us. "Oh, nice you came. You heard we get one baby boy?"

"Auntie told. She coming for see you, too. We ran. Only slow she walks."

"Not suppose to talk about Auntie like that. What if she hear? Need show respect."

Taizo nodded obediently beside me.

"When you coming home?" I asked. "Today?"

"I like but no can. Doctor tell me stay one week, like that. Everybody who gets baby need for stay in bed."

The door to Mom's room opened, and Auntie stepped inside. She set down the potted orchid she had carried from home and walked to my mother's bed.

"How you stay?" she asked.

"Good. No need bring nothing."

"Small, that. Only small. How baby?"

"Try look. Can sit this side." Mom moved over in her bed to make room for Auntie and picked up the baby that had been lying beside her. I hadn't even noticed him. Now she held him with cradled arms. Auntie sat alongside her on the bed and they talked about how much the baby looked like my father.

"Same-same," Auntie said.

"Yes, same."

"The eyes, I think."

"Yes, maybe the eyes."

At the time I couldn't understand comparisons between an infant and a man. In later years, the physical similarities between the two would always startle me.

Auntie reached over and rubbed William's arm from elbow to wrist. She also touched my mother's arm and, comfortable with this familiarity, neither woman withdrew.

"You like hold him?" asked Mom.

Auntie accepted the baby from my mother. "Try look," she said. "William get lucky ears." She peered at my mother's head. "You get ears like this, or what?"

"Not me," Mom said. "My ears only stay flat. That kind teacup ears. Lucky, those ears."

Auntie held the baby the length of her outstretched arms, tilting his head with her hands. "I think can balance one coin on these ears. Baby going be rich someday."

"Too good somebody going be rich," my mother said and took William back into her arms.

Auntie stood to go, brushing the bed as if to smooth the memory. "The baby one boy," she said with a strange gentleness.

"Yes, one boy."

"Sorry, Mariko."

"Not your fault," my mother told her and tears fell from her cheeks to her baby's. Auntie returned to the bed and they hugged for a long time, the baby pressed between them. Mom and Auntie cried long, deep sobs with arms wrapped together. Taizo and I looked at each other, puzzled. I couldn't understand who was comforting whom. Now, more than forty years later, I still do not know.

Mom must have suddenly remembered we were there. She let go of Auntie and said to us, "Go home already. No forget, now. Behave for Auntie."

Taizo and I both nodded our assent. I guess he didn't feel like talking any more than I because neither of us said a word. Instead he took my hand and led me away from the hospital.

We began walking toward Auntie's house. As we continued on, holding hands, I tried to figure out why Mom and Auntie had been sad. What had I missed? I looked up at Taizo's face, ready to ask him, and he shook his head to keep me quiet. He wouldn't allow me any questions, so I held even more tightly to his hand. I know he was only two years older than I, but that hand brought some comfort to a most perplexing day.

A few months prior to William's birth, my paternal grandfather died in our sewing room. He had arrived four years earlier after my grandma's death and spent much of this four years in the bed that my parents wedged alongside the sewing machine. When I asked my mother why Grandpa lay around in bed all the time, she answered that grief had sent him there, as if such an emotion is easier to bear beneath covers. He would move his feet aside for me, and I would sit on the end of his bed to watch Mother's fingers guide denim and cotton into shirts and pants, dresses and overalls. When she ran low on store-bought fabric, she used hundred-pound rice bags bleached by the sun. The two of them talked in Japanese, my grandfather more rapidly than my mother, and I understood little save the inflections, the sighs,

33

and the humming between Grandpa's gritted teeth. Grandpa had a way of returning to old stories, and the ensuing hum strengthened with each telling. I feared that hum because I could hear Grandpa fighting to control it.

"Grandma never like die Hawaii," my mother would turn and translate for me. "She wanted for die Japan." And as she translated, Grandpa would hum.

We all knew when my grandfather was nearing his death because his senses began to disappear, fading after a lifetime. At first he could no longer smell the food my mother brought him on his wooden tray and left his triangular bowl of rice untouched. Then, when his eyes failed, he couldn't see the pictures I colored for him.

"Can go talk Grandpa?" my mother would ask me.

"No can talk him. He no can understand English."

"Never mind," she said. "He only like hear you talk. The words not going matter."

I dutifully spoke to him in English, and he answered me in Japanese. Gradually I moved farther up the length of his bed, and near the end of his life I settled alongside his waist and studied his empty eyes. Because neither of us understood the other's language, we spoke in a backward pattern: if he laughed, I then said something funny so that the laughter made sense. About two weeks into these mixed-language conversations came the day when I startled Grandpa at his bedside. He had not heard my approaching footsteps, and a few days later, he couldn't hear me talk. He was a man closing unto himself.

Yet through all of this he managed a dignity because old age didn't take my grandpa's sense of touch. His bony hand, a hand that had held more sugar cane than children, gripped mine until I wanted to run from him. Grandpa was dying, and I felt that he tried to pull me along with him as he coaxed my hip further onto his bed. A man who had spent a lifetime avoiding the touch of others, he now held my hand against time. I looked down at his sun-wrinkled hand wrapped around mine and imagined all the Maui rains funneling down its grooves. He held my hand firmly so that I couldn't let go. If I turned my head to look out the window to where Taizo played, the hand tightened.

That's why I was the first to know when my grandfather died. With my hand in his, I felt him let go of me.

After Grandpa changed worlds, I gradually understood his desperation for touch. To this day I can visualize my grandfather, a hard-working Oriental too long in the sun, and if I concentrate, I can also still hear him. Although I cannot at will summon his smell, that mixture of incense, burning cane, and the subtle neutrality of rice, there are times when I happen upon that smell and remember Grandpa. All these years later, I can still visualize him, hear him, even smell him, but I can no longer feel my hand in his. His weathered touch, desperate to hold onto a little boy's hand, left with my grandpa's final heartbeat.

I think my mother also understood this loss of touch. A few

months after my grandpa's death, when she carried William home from the hospital after his birth, she seemed to hold him against time. Her arms cradled the baby, lowering him only to change the cotton diaper and even then resting one hand beneath his black hair.

The baby napped on the bed beneath my mother's arm. Only when she needed to use the bathroom did she release him to his cradle.

"Come, Spencer. Mommy going bathroom. Can rock baby in cradle?"

"Can," I said, crouching at the cradle's far end.

"This way," she said, demonstrating.

"This way, Mommy?"

"Too hard, that . . . there, that's how. Not hard."

Together we rocked the baby's cradle. My mom's hands touched the cradle gently, easily. "You rocked me like this?" I asked, understanding I was once small enough to fit in the cradle.

She shook her head. "Never had cradle then."

"Can try now?"

"Try what? You think can fit inside cradle? Take care brother now. Mommy come back soon."

She left the room and William cried. His face got puffy and red. I rocked his cradle and tried to will him to quiet down.

"There, there," Mom said to William when she returned from the bathroom. "No need cry. Going be okay."

"I rocked him same like you said."

"I know, Spencer. Mommy know."

She nursed him upon her chest, and William reached for her breast the same way a baby bird stretches his wobbly neck toward the mother bird. The mechanics of breastfeeding intrigued me. When I got close enough to study the repetitive tug of William's cheeks, my mother pulled away her upper blouse so I could see better. Nearly asleep, eyes closed, the baby sucked and let go, sucked and let go. William's mouth, the last of his body to fall asleep, relaxed into a slightly open circle. He lay with his head tucked into the curve of her breast, and milk droplets fell from his mouth.

As I knelt beside Mom's chair, her hand reached past the sleeping baby and rubbed from the front of my head to the back, continuing in a circle upward along my neck and onto my cheeks. "You one good boy," she said to me. "Good if William come same like you."

Our eyes returned to William. His mouth held that same open circle, poised near her nipple as if he wanted to be ready in case he got hungry anytime soon. Finally, as I watched, he fell all the way into sleep, past hunger or even memory of hunger, and his tiny mouth closed.

"Where Taizo stay?" I asked, one brother reminding me of the other.

"Outside," my mother said.

"Can go outside?"

"Can. No get in Daddy's way, but. He working in the garden."

"I not going bother Daddy. Only like for find Taizo."

Led by the tinkling of metal, I found my brother crafting a silver ring beneath the front-yard plumeria tree. He and I made silver rings whenever we had a rare extra quarter, tapping the rounded side of a heavy teaspoon against the coin's rim. Thousands and thousands of taps would flatten and widen the rim until we could drill a center hole, file the ring smooth, and polish it shiny.

We were each about halfway finished with our current rings. I crawled beneath the tree, pulled the teaspoon and quarter from my pocket, and started tapping with Taizo.

Dad was picking soybeans in the vegetable garden when Uncle Toshi arrived. The two men often visited each other's homes or gardens, and I rarely paid them much attention. Dad straightened from his bean-picking stoop, and the two brothers, normally relaxed with conversation, didn't greet each other.

Dad's strength and sharp body lines contrasted to Uncle's softer angles. Seeing them together, it didn't seem possible the two men were brothers. My father's bold eyes and rigid body challenged; Uncle gave in. When I drew them with crayons, I chose gray for my uncle. For Dad I chose glistening black.

"I think you going come today," my father said to his brother. Something was wrong with my father's tone: the current of his voice felt dangerous, ominous, capable of pulling a grown man out to sea.

"I going already," said Uncle.

"No need go away. You came."

"I came, true. Maybe I wrong for come."

"You came," my father said again. "No can be like never came."

My uncle tilted his head toward the ground. "Wrong?" he asked my father. "Was wrong for come?"

"Not wrong." Dad looked up toward the sun. "Come," he said, indicating with his head toward the front porch. "Too hot this side. More better talk there."

The two men crossed the yard carefully parallel to each other. Dad, the elder, walked straight, matter-of-fact, whereas Uncle proceeded with more caution, a man of perpetually bent knees. They climbed the front stairs and then separated to opposite sides of the porch.

Uncle looked across the porch toward Dad, but my father did not look in return. Instead he pressed both hands upon the porch rail and leaned forward, his upper body stretched beyond the porch, neck strained, and he would have been looking straight at Taizo and me if he had only noticed.

Taizo, undisturbed, continued his methodical tapping. My own hand slowed to a selective beat as I attempted to tap against the rhythm of the men's words.

"I never tell Sachi I coming," my uncle said of his wife. "Can still change mind." He talked to the side of my father's face. "Already tell Mariko?" he asked carefully.

"She know," my father said.

Taizo must have been listening because his tapping slowed before resuming at a quicker pace, the same as my startled heartbeat. More boldly, now, I looked straight at my father. He gazed blankly in our direction. I don't think he knew we were listening, and if he did know, he didn't care. Dad wasn't one to worry about a child's thoughts.

For a short while neither man spoke. Uncle looked at Dad, but Dad looked past the porch rail, past the gallon jars of Mom's salted lemons cooking in the sun.

"Hiroshi," my uncle said, "no need talk. I going home like I never came."

My father pushed back from the porch rail and straightened. His shoulders bent neither forward nor backward; he stood clearly in the present. All was quiet except for Taizo's eerie tapping. Uncle stood still, defeated.

Dad folded his arms and looked to the skies. His jaw drew rigid. He stood absolutely still, looking into the distance. Some years later I would learn there is nowhere further away than deep within oneself. Perhaps that is where my father looked that day.

"Never mind," said Uncle. "I going now. Pretend I never came."

My father's body shook. Quickly, control regained, my father said, "The boy yours."

"My boy?"

Dad pivoted and faced Uncle. My father's face was expressionless. The ability to subdue outward emotion had been passed down from his ancestors as surely as blood and bones. "Your boy," he assured my uncle. "Mariko going bring him. Go home already."

Dad, without another word, walked down the stairs and over to the garden. He was bent over the soybeans when Uncle hurried away from our yard.

Taizo stopped tapping. He dropped the teaspoon and leaned back onto his palms. I waited for him to speak and discredit all I had heard, and instead he breathed in, breathed out, rocking on the palms of his hands, and when he angled his head toward me I knew from his face that I had gotten it right. Dad had given William to Uncle Toshi. At the price of a baby's love, the older brother was sacrificing for the younger. Uncle and Auntie would no longer be childless.

Taizo led me inside toward William—we would see him while we could—and we stepped out of our slippers before going inside. He led me to the inner corner of the room and we sat on the floor, he on one side of the angle and I on the other. Our legs crisscrossed each other's near the knees. William was awake now, and Mom held him against her shoulder in the koa chair.

I heard the back door open and close and could picture Dad dropping stalks of soybeans onto the kitchen table, but the task took longer than usual. The sound of my father's solid bare footsteps preceded him down the hall and into the parlor. Mom, who usually acknowledged Dad upon arrival, ignored him.

He crossed the room and sat on the couch. "Toshi came," he said, looking at my mother.

"I heard."

"You heard?"

"Only some."

Pain is audible. Those who can't hear its poignant edge do not listen. I wondered if my father refused to hear my mother's pain.

"Pau already," Dad said, choosing the Hawaiian word to tell my mother it was all over, past the possibility that he would change his mind.

My mother's arms tightened their hold on the baby. "Only been one week I give birth. Please Hiroshi. I still get blood from baby."

My father said nothing in reply.

"You no can do this."

Again, he said nothing.

"I been one good mother."

Nothing.

"No can say nothing. No can take away and never say nothing."

His head hung back and his hands pushed against his thighs. "Toshi stay wait long time already."

"Our baby, but. I not going bring him. Why you never give him?"

"No. More better you bring him."

"Can wait little while."

"No can."

"Only little while."

He shook his head. "Go already."

Mother continued to rock William as he lay across her arms. After a while I noticed that she rocked, too. She slowed and her lowered head lay on her knees.

"This my boy," she said beneath fallen hair. She raised her head, her eyes flashed, and this time she said more loudly, "My son, I telling you."

Dad shook his head.

"No shake head. This my boy."

"No more."

I watched my mother. Hate took away all the life from her face.

"He my boy," she said beneath pale eyes. "This my little boy. So no say nothing. Why you no can understand this my boy? I only like for be one mother, not like the kind wants fancy things."

"No make hard," my father said.

"Hard? Why you say that? I no see you get hard time." She yelled, "You no can take away. This baby mine."

She held William as if she were guarding him, a mother's

child safe from a father's reach. "I not going let you take," she warned, and as soon as she said this she must have realized that it was no use because she began to wail.

When she quieted, she lay her head against the back of the chair. More calmly now, she spoke as if detached from her feelings. "You no love the boy," she said. "How can the father no love the son?" She had lost her challenge and spoke more to herself than to my father.

He stood from the couch and between gritted teeth he said to my mother, "No say I never love him. He get the father's blood. Nothing going change that. So no say nothing. Nothing!"

My mother, concerned about her husband, looked toward him with kinder eyes. "But look, Hiroshi. He looks all over you."

"He no look nothing like me," my father said, sitting back onto the couch.

"Hiroshi, but——"

"Nothing. We no look nothing alike."

"He your boy."

"No."

She stretched her baby-filled arms toward Dad. "Try hold."

"No can. I no can."

"Never get government papers. No can get adoption without government papers. Need government papers."

"What for? Government papers? Who need government papers? Only humbug, that. No, no need. No need government papers. One promise, this."

"Suppose to get."

"No need. The name no even change—still going be William Susumu Fujii. See? No need government papers."

Dad remained home while Mom carried William to his new parents. Taizo and I walked with my mother, and I remember watching her face, a study in browns, and asking her when William would come back.

"He not coming back," my mother said. "Can see every time but not coming back for live."

"Oh," I said. "You going give me Auntie too?"

"No, Spencer. Not going."

"Daddy going give me Auntie?"

"No worry, Spencer. Daddy not going do that."

I wanted to believe my mother, and after a few years I finally would.

The walk to Auntie's would have taken a few minutes, except that we stopped beneath the silver oak tree. It was my mother's favorite tree; she loved the bark pastels. "Try look," she would tell me whenever we passed by. "Plenty trees get fancy flowers and leaves. Too noisy, them. Get tired all that noise. More better you learn for be same like this tree."

On this day she said nothing as she looked at the pinks and greens of the trunk. She lifted William toward the sky and lowered him so their faces met, breath upon breath, and then my mother rested her face next to William's stomach.

I sat next to Taizo in the shade of the tree. From there we watched my mother unwrap William's patchwork blanket and spread it beneath the tree's shade. What she did next I never understood.

She took off all of William's clothes, including his diaper, and lay him naked on his back atop the blanket. The baby drew in his knees and elbows, tight and fearful, and Mom lay alongside him, head beside head. Harbored by the oak's branches, she simply looked at her little boy. Her eyes studied William's body and, then, supported by an elbow, she stroked her naked little boy's feet.

Taizo and I watched cross-legged and holding hands. I did not think of speaking.

Next my mother knelt beside William's body and bowed across his tiny stomach. "Be one kind, honest boy," she said, and that undoubtedly encompassed all of her expectations. Family tradition held that it was unfortunate to be stupid, but unforgivable to be dishonest.

The wind strengthened across William's body; my mother reclothed him. Then we were again on our way and momentarily reached Auntie Sachi's back door.

"Sachi . . . Sachi," my mother called up the steps.

Auntie, no doubt respectful of my mother's grief, opened the door slowly, easing into the sadness. She closed the door behind her, and the two women looked at each other.

"Bring William," my mother said.

"Yes," said Auntie.

"Likes for drink plenty milk."

"I get plenty."

"Only likes for sleep on stomach."

This time Auntie only nodded.

"Going forgive you," my mother said. She looked down at the son in her arms. She cradled him. She rocked him. She kissed one foot and then the other. To William she said, "I going try forgive you. Only can try."

With these words, her arms stretched up the steps toward Auntie with a mother's offering. Auntie also reached, and for a moment William lay in the arms of both women. But then my mother's arms fell empty to her side, and William lay in Auntie's arms. Mom turned her back and hurried off with Taizo and me each beneath an arm.

"No worry, Mom," I said as we walked. "When William grow up, I can tell him."

"No, son, no can. No can ever talk this day. Only if Uncle and Auntie like tell."

We reached home and found Dad in the parlor. He was looking over the back of the couch, out the window, and did not at first acknowledge our return. Slowly, then, he turned, and my mother said, "Hiroshi . . . you been crying?"

I looked at my father's face and wondered why Mom thought he had been crying. I couldn't tell from looking at him. My father said nothing to confirm or deny her observation.

"Hiroshi," she said, shaking her head, "I never seen you cry."

Dad visibly straightened. "Still never," he said.

Mom's hands pressed against her breasts, and her arms pressed into her chest. "My milk," she said, puzzled. "Only full with William's milk."

"Get two more boys," my father said.

"Look how big already."

"Going need you. Always going need you."

"They growing big already," she said.

Dad walked toward the hallway. In the door frame he pivoted and spoke to my mother, "Baby look same like me."

"Same-same," Mom softly agreed.

With that acknowledged, Dad left the room.

"Time for cook rice," my mother said, and now Taizo and I were alone in the parlor. He walked to the shelf and pulled down his cloth bag of marbles. We knelt and he dropped the marbles onto the wooden floor.

"Can have one?" I asked.

"Can."

"Any kind?"

He thought for a moment and shook his head. "Not any kind," he decided. "Some I like keep."

He studied the marbles and chose a clear marble ribboned with orange for my outstretched hand.

"The other hand needs one marble," I said, figuring it was worth a try.

"Can have," Taizo decided. "Can pick any kind this time."

"Any kind?"

"Can. Go pick."

"Only today or for keep?" I asked.

"For keep," said Taizo.

Usually the blue marbles would have attracted me because blue reminded me of sky and ocean. Today that expansiveness frightened me. I eliminated blues from my selection. Green marbles pulled me into a feeling of peaceful cane fields. Green would make a good choice. One marble was a soft, blurry green, suggesting cane on a windy day, and another rivaled the iridescence of a mejiro bird. But, as it turned out, I didn't pick any of the green marbles. My selection, in the end, was much simpler.

I had spotted one plain marble that looked nearly identical to the marble Taizo had already given me, a clear marble ribboned with orange. I chose that marble and clicked it against its matching mate.

"Same-same?" asked Taizo, his eyes wide. "You wanted for pick same-same?"

"Yes," I said, "like one family."

"Family not always same."

"This two stay brothers," I said.

"Us not same-same."

"Try look," I said, holding the marbles in front of him. With them balanced between thumbs and forefingers, I again clicked them. "Same-same. Brothers."

I lay on my back with one marble in each hand and then held them above my head toward the ceiling. I tried to look through them. I turned the marbles and imagined the ribbons were floating in the wind. One of the marbles clearly had more nicks than the other but even a young boy knows that physical markings are only a partial explanation.

As I lay there on my back, I felt Taizo place the soles of his feet against mine in a childhood game. He lay opposite me on the floor in mirror image.

"You like play?" I asked him.

He responded by pushing his right leg straight, bending my opposing left leg.

"Good fun," I told him, straightening my bent knee and bending his.

"Try two legs same time," he said, and together we managed a rhythm. We alternated so that at any one time we each bent one leg and straightened the other.

Back and forth, back and forth. That's how Taizo and I went forward into the afternoon. We were two brothers, touching.

The next afternoon my mother sat with an arm around me on the back steps. She pressed her other arm against her upper chest. Dad was gone, working in the cane fields. We sat quietly, thinking, until my mother began to hum. It was the first time I'd ever heard her hum, and immediately brought to mind my grandpa's escalating hum. I looked guardedly at her, afraid that she also would lose control, but she smiled.

"Get scissors for Mommy," she said.

"Scissors?" I asked.

She nodded. "Sewing scissors. Can bring for me?"

"Can," I said. I ran inside the house and retrieved them from her sewing table. "Here," I offered, returning outside.

"Go play," she said. She stared at the scissors and then opened and closed them as if cutting the air.

"What the scissors for?" I asked, leaning away from their points.

"Never mind." She laid the scissors down on the steps. "Need for cut something."

"I like watch."

"No. Go play. Maybe can find Taizo for play with."

I hesitated. She nodded once, very deliberately. I walked down the steps and looked back over my shoulder as I rounded the side of the house. She waved me on.

I did not go play. Instead I entered the house through our front door and ran to the kitchen, pulling back the curtain from the open window, where I watched as she lifted single strands of hair and cut them. She hummed quietly as she cut, one strand, another, carefully separating each hair and cutting it at the root.

She began to hum more loudly and was no longer so careful about separating the single strands. Her fingers impatiently grabbed. She cut further away from her scalp, no longer following the hair to its roots. I covered my ears with my hands and held the curtain open with my elbow.

She reached with both hands behind her head, and I watched the clumps of long hair slide down her back and settle in a circle around her body. She cut all the length from her hair, cropping it near her ears, before she dropped the scissors to the steps.

Finished, she lay down on her back, knees bent. Her hands groped near her waist for the hair she had cut, and she gathered it in a pile on her stomach.

She didn't appear to notice me as she carried her pile of hair through the kitchen and down the hallway. I followed her into her bedroom and watched as she lay the hair on my father's pillow.

"Why?" I asked.

She shook her head. When she spoke, her voice sounded very tired. "Not suppose to watch. Suppose to go play."

"I no feel like playing."

"Then go read. Do something."

I pulled down a book from the shelf and read in the parlor until my father returned home from work. He pulled off his boots on the front porch, and said nothing to my mother when she met him at the door. His cheeks tightened, and then he strode past her to get a change of clothes from his bedroom to wear after his daily furo bath.

He came back out of the room holding the pillow in his outstretched arms. "What for?" he demanded of my mother. "What for cut hair?"

"Just happen," she said.

"No can just happen," he told her. He shook the pillow and the hair spilled onto our wooden floor. "Need for sweep," he said, throwing the pillow to the chair.

I interjected quietly, "I can sweep."

He whirled toward me. Between gritted teeth he ordered, "Leave it. Your mother going sweep." He got his clothes and headed to the furo bath. My mother went to the kitchen, but didn't come back with the broom.

The hair lay strewn on our parlor floor for days. We walked over it, around it, avoiding it as much as possible, but still we tracked it on our bare feet to our rooms, our beds. Finally one morning the hair was gone, swept in the dark of night. I don't know who swept it.

As the weeks passed, it grew natural for me to see William in Auntie's arms. She often sat in our parlor with William upon her lap as she visited with my mother. Each woman pretended, without a hint to the contrary, that William had been born to Auntie.

My mother deferred to Auntie's love for William. "He no like me carry. He only want you," my mother said as she handed over the crying baby. They were so convincing that I began to wonder how they had forgotten the truth.

William was a fearful infant. Taizo and I called him a scarecrow. He huddled in his mother's lap, his arms and legs gathered toward his body as if touching the wooden floor might be dangerous. In his earliest months he wouldn't let either me or Taizo near him.

When William learned halfway through his first year to crawl, he became more daring. He began to crawl nearer and nearer Taizo and me until he was climbing over our outstretched legs. If we weren't in the same room with him, he searched for us. He crawled away from his mother and found Taizo and me at the kitchen table or in our bedroom, playing cards on the floor. He crawled through the middle of our card games, and the cards stuck to the sweat on his legs. If we were playing marbles instead of cards, he popped them in his mouth when he thought we weren't looking. His visits could exasperate me. He especially liked crawling to the bathroom to pester the chicks that Dad was raising under a light bulb. We were all supposed to close the door to the bathroom when William was around.

As he neared his first birthday, I watched him learn to walk between the two women. Mom and Auntie kneeled on zabuton pillows in our parlor. Their hands alternately lured him. He shuffled to my mom, turned around, and returned to Auntie. Back and forth he walked.

"Come to me," I called, kneeling. "Can come."

He looked right at me and then walked to Taizo instead. Taizo carefully turned William toward me. "Try call him again," he directed.

"Come, William," I said. "I not going let you fall."

He watched me, deciding. He looked at his mom.

She nodded. "Go on. Can make it."

I leaned my body toward him so that I could shorten the distance between us. "Come, William. Come."

He walked straight to me with short, tripping steps. I caught him.

By the time William turned three years old, he relied heavily on the idea that I would catch him when needed. He balanced fearlessly on my shoulders to reach the lowest branch of his backyard ohia tree, while beneath him I absorbed his sway. He let me pull off his Band-Aids. I slowly peeled back the adhesives and watched William's skin pucker. When Taizo and I visited his home, he was happiest to see me. He liked Taizo, but only for me did he empty his pockets and hands. He offered me half-chewed pieces of dried shrimp and accidentally stepped on my ankles.

Our days were ordinary days, and in Japanese Camp we were ordinary children. The three of us climbed the ohia tree, shot marbles, invented card games, played milk covers, and walked as far as we wanted. When William fell down his front porch steps, Taizo and I sat on either side of him.

"I like see," I said, carefully moving his hands away from his scraped knee.

Taizo leaned over the knee and studied the scrape. "Not bad," he decided. "No even bleed."

"Hurts, but," William insisted, again hiding the scrape with his cupped hands.

"Only at first," I assured him. "Not going hurt for long time."

He looked at me suspiciously. "How you know?"

"I stay older than you," I said.

"Oh," he answered, satisfied. In those early years it was explanation enough for the both of us.

William depended upon me, and I depended upon Taizo. Ever since William's birth, Taizo and I had become close again. He patiently gave me his time. Some days we didn't want William tagging along at his slower pace. On those occasions Taizo and I headed out together, carefully avoiding William's row of homes.

Taizo and I whittled guava branch slingshots with his pocket-knife and practiced shooting rocks at avocados, which we called pears. The most heavily fruited avocado tree was in the large expanse of grass between Filipino and Chinese Camps.

The pears also made ideal bombs when we played war. Their green flesh spattered graphically. We played war until Mr. Chong from Chinese Camp invariably discovered what we were up to and shooed us away in rapid Chinese. We knew he wanted to use the pears for pig feed. Back then, I didn't know of a single human being who actually ate avocados.

Common ginger plants grew abundantly in our woods. Taizo and I yanked off the large buds to make loud, high-pitched whistles. We each pulled a leaf from the layered bud and folded it in half. Then, folds out, we gritted the leaves between our front teeth and blew. As long as we stayed in the woods, no one made us stop.

The two of us often took aimless walks together. As we walked, we chewed long strands of grass until the blades turned black. We wandered until all of a sudden we found ourselves in the woods, looking down from the branches of a banyan tree, or on the beach, skipping stones across waves. It wasn't until after Taizo died that I realized the walk itself had also been a destination, a place to be reached.

"Look," he said on one of the many days we walked down the main road that ran among Wainoa cane fields. "The cane grew plenty already."

I tilted my head, considering. "Taller than me, I think."

"Try stand that side," said Taizo, indicating with his hand. "Can measure." I ran across the road and stood with my back to the cane field. Taizo folded his arms and shook his head. "Not yet," he said. "You still more tall."

We compared ourselves against the cane each time we passed that field. Soon the cane was taller than even Taizo. It grew until we could no longer see past it. That was a rainy year and the cane grew bushy tassles.

We tasted the sugar. Taizo cut off a short length of stalk with his pocketknife, and we took turns chewing the juice from it. One end of the stalk was his, and the other end was mine. We turned the stalk each time it passed between us. Then we got confused and didn't know whether we had turned it or not. We tried to figure out whose end was whose by studying the teeth marks, but in the end we didn't care.

We visited that particular field until the months became nearly two years. One day Taizo looked at the field and slowly nodded. "Getting ready for burn," he said.

"How can tell?" I asked quietly, looking up at my older brother's face.

"Look how brown. Went turn off the water already."

I looked closely. The tops of the stalks were turning yellow-brown and leaves hung limply. "Why?" I asked him. "Why they turn off the water?"

Taizo considered and put his hand on my shoulder. "More easy for burn," he said.

I sighed. After nearly two years of irrigating the cane, the plantation had now shut off the water. The cane that Taizo and I had measured ourselves against was ready for harvesting. The flames would ignite anything unharvestable. Leaves, insects, and rodents would sizzle.

The cane that Taizo and I had pretended would live forever had reached its prime. My father, I knew, would help to set the fire. He would get up at night, and the next day there would be black soot all over my mother's windows.

Two nights later, Taizo and I lay listening as my dad got up in the dark. We heard him searching for the red kerchief he needed across his mouth to protect against smoke inhalation. My mother found it for him. We heard the front door bang shut as he headed toward the field. We were determined to watch this fire, to see the flames travel the rows of our field. Taizo and I walked to the window to wait.

Spencer," said Taizo, shaking me awake. I had fallen asleep on the floor beneath the window. "Wake up."

I pulled myself up to the windowsill and looked outside. My eyesight was blurry, and I blinked rapidly to clear it. The fire in the distance was burning our field. The colors of that night were orange, black, red, yellow. The fire was much taller than the tallest cane. It appeared to me as if the sky, rather than the cane field, was on fire. The flames lit up the clouds, and I began to smell smoke.

"Gone," I told Taizo, my hands on the windowsill. "The field gone."

He nodded. "Gone already."

"Tomorrow can go look?"

"Can."

"The smoke smells stink."

"Quiet already. Just watch."

I shook my head, having seen enough. My hands pushed away from the windowsill, and I crawled back into bed. To make sure I would see no more fire that night, to make absolutely certain, I shut my eyes tightly and pulled the covers above my head. Still, I could smell the smoke as the cane collapsed into the fire. I knew the smell of burning cane.

The smells of cane were those of dirt, poison, and smoke. In its prime, the field smelled of dirt. In its death, smoke. Between, there were the smells of poison. On some of those occasions, the plantation sprayed our neighborhoods along with the cane fields. A truck slowly drove up and down the rows of our camps as it sprayed DDT from a huge canister.

"Get ready," my mother shouted. "Truck stay coming."

I ran nervously in circles, knowing what that meant. "I no like," I called to my mother. "I no like."

"No can help," she said. "Need for kill bugs." She gathered Taizo and me into a circle. "Close eyes."

The fog of poison passed through our open windows, beneath our doors. I closed my eyes tightly. I couldn't hold my breath long enough and had to inhale. I could taste the poison in the back of my throat, and my mouth watered. I swallowed once, twice. Gradually the air began to clear, and we continued with our day as if nothing unusual had happened.

Following the spray, we found long, dead centipedes; upside-down roaches; and cane spiders, as big as a hand when alive, shrunken in death. The scorpions were more rare, but I recognized their curved tails. Dead ants were everywhere. When my mother swept them up, they stuck to the bristles of her broom.

Even the periodic poison couldn't control the ants. They chewed through sealed cereal boxes and drank water from our kitchen sink. They nested inside our towels, boxes, and mattresses. My mother once found a huge nest inside a many-folded sheet. She held it open so I could watch thousands of ants circle a queen and a pile of cooked rice.

"Where they get rice?" I asked her, amazed that ants liked rice as much as my family did.

"The floor, the rubbish. No can stop ants."

The insects crawled around in the dark. If I had to use the bathroom at night, I stepped gingerly, touching the floor with only my toes. I closed my eyes when I first turned on the bathroom light so the insects could safely hide. Flying roaches startled me. I swung wildly at them, hoping I'd miss.

One night I awoke abruptly. My arm tingled painfully. I batted at my brother with my other arm.

"Go sleep," he mumbled.

I batted harder. "Arm hurts," I told him. "Get bit."

After he turned on the light, we spotted a six-inch creature near my thigh. "Centipede," I shouted, scrambling from bed. Taizo ran for our parents while I stared at the two-pronged mark near the crook of my elbow. The tingling sensation felt similar to an arm that's been slept upon awkwardly, hindering blood circulation, but the pain was tremendously magnified. I didn't fear dying because I'd never heard of anyone dying from a centipede bite. A boy at school, though, had missed a couple of weeks when the bite on his toe became severely infected, and a centipede bite was glamorous after-the-fact, the way it got showed off at the schoolyard.

Our entire family gathered in my room. Mom rubbed a baking soda paste on my sore arm, a folk remedy that gave mothers a plan of action, even if ineffective, while Dad smashed the centipede with a rubber slipper. He kneed the bed away from the wall and pumped bug poison along the floorboards. There must have been a nest in the wall. The next day we killed six baby centipedes as they crawled across our bedroom floor. Taizo and I wore slippers inside the house for a week.

"Over there," I told him as we settled for bed a couple of

weeks later. He sat upright beside me on the bed and waited for me to continue. "Get one centipede on the wall," I showed him, pointing.

"One mark, that," he said. "One crayon mark."

"You sure?"

"Am," he said.

I wanted to believe him, but even big brothers can make mistakes. I studied the mark in case it moved. I watched until it was too dark in the room to see the mark clearly, and then I decided I might as well believe Taizo. He somehow knew things I didn't. Those were the years when Taizo and I were close. I have tried to figure out why it changed, although I believe I know when.

The memory conjures the smell of fresh paint, a powerful smell that crinkled my forehead. Taizo and I knelt across from each other on our bedroom floor, carefully distant from the wet walls. Trade winds swept boldly through our curtainless window and cooled the back of my neck.

"You get plenty milk covers," I said, noting the height of the pile by Taizo's knee.

"I won Fred."

"Fred easy for win," I said. "He no can aim."

Taizo and I had long been saving milk covers from the bottles our milkman delivered. Each morning we poured extra milk into our cereal to accumulate them more quickly. This game required each player to add an equal number of the cardboard disks to a stack on the ground. We then took turns throwing our "lucky" milk cover at the stack. A player got to keep any milk covers that flipped over.

Taizo placed three milk covers in a vertical stack between us.

"Three?" I said. "I only get five. What if lose?"

"You like play or not?" he asked.

I added three milk covers to the stack. Taizo won the toss and got to go first. He threw his milk cover at the pile and all six milk covers flipped over.

"You win," I quietly said. Only the week before I had had twenty-three milk covers. Now I was down to my last two, which I stacked in the middle. Taizo added two of his own, first shaking them in a lucky way.

I won the toss and got first chance, slamming my milk cover but missing the pile. Taizo took a turn and only the top milk cover flipped over. He added that to the collection at his knee. We continued, the other three milk covers yet to be won, until Taizo got them all with a solid hit.

"No fair," I said. "You cheat."

"Sore sport."

"So, but not fair. Cheater."

Dad walked into the room. I hadn't known he was in the house. I felt dizzy and nauseous. The paint fumes further sickened me. "Get problem?" he asked angrily.

Taizo and I kept quiet.

"Somebody cheat, or what? You, Taizo, what? Somebody cheat?"

"No," he said, looking down.

"What then?" He looked straight at me. "Telling stories, boy?"

"I never mean it," I said.

"Call somebody one name and never mean it?"

"Sorry."

"Too late for sorry. More better you think. Hold out one hand."

I held my hand toward Dad.

"Not me," he said, shaking his head. "Taizo."

"Taizo?" I asked. "Taizo going hit me?"

"Hurry already," Dad warned.

I held my hand toward Taizo and watched his face tighten. I knew he didn't want to slap my hand. Two boys get caught in the tangles of tradition and can't get out.

Taizo looked at Dad. "Have to?" he asked.

"Hurry already. Spencer need learn."

Taizo reached over and slapped my hand.

"There," Dad said, turning to leave. "Some shame, Spencer. Look what you make brother do." He shook his head and left the room.

We sat quietly for a few minutes before Taizo said to me, "You like try find mango?"

I nodded.

"I had for do it."

"I know."

We left the house together and did find mango that day. Taizo climbed the tree and tossed the fruit down to me. We sat back to back behind the old store. Our shoulder blades rubbed, and I laid back my head into the groove at Taizo's neck. We smelled of sweat and mango juice. We must have eaten about four mangoes each. It seemed we were going to be okay.

That's why I didn't understand what happened to Taizo in the ensuing months and years. He drew back from me, all the way back, and I refused to let go, refused to give up, the same way I had years earlier. Before I could understand where it came from, Taizo was drawing imaginary lines down the center of our double bed and walking apart from me so that our swinging arms never brushed. He refused to wake up and watch cane fires. He wouldn't let me borrow his pocketknife. When I dared to put my hand in his, he scolded me. "Too big for hold hands," he said. He remained kind to me, but he took away the intimacy.

I began to spend more time with William. He walked close to me. He followed me. I could choose when. Taizo had so rarely smiled that I appreciated William's grin.

He loved to count out loud as he climbed steps or lined up his marbles. I asked him to stop, and he began counting in whispers. "Never mind," I said after a few days of listening to him whisper. "Can count loud."

One morning we sat at his kitchen table. I was about nine years old and William half that. Auntie Sachi was rolling sushi at the far end of the table, and the kitchen smelled like vinegar. William lay the side of his face down on the table. I copied him. We talked face to face from a sideward view.

"Your ears stick out," I said. One of his ears lay pressed against the table, and the other ear stuck out.

"Cannot help it."

"Nobody get ears like yours," I said.

"Never mind. Mom says lucky I get." He looked toward his mom for confirmation. "Right?" he asked her.

Auntie laughed. "Only lucky, your ears. Can be rich someday." She went to the sink and turned on the water.

"Nothing lucky about ears that stick out," I quietly told William.

"So. Never mind. Anyway, you get one crooked smile."

"Not," I said.

"Does. Looks plenty crooked."

"Not."

"Looks crooked to me."

"You stay sideways," I reminded him. "Everything looks crooked from sideways."

Auntie's hands reached between our heads and set a bowl of lychee fruit on the table. I picked one from the bowl and peeled the bumpy red skin.

William grabbed a handful and counted them out loud at my elbow. He grouped them in a line from smallest to largest, studied them at eye level, switched two lychee, studied them again, and nodded.

Then he formed lychee "families." "One baby lychee," he said, holding up the tiniest fruit.

I nodded, uninterested. William decided three small lychee were the children, the four biggest were fathers, and eleven average-sized lychee were mothers.

He divided his fruits into two distinct groups and returned about half to the bowl. The two groups of lychee were piled in front of him. He called one group, "Auntie Mariko, Uncle Hiroshi, Taizo, and Spencer." The other group was "Dad, Mom, and baby William."

I was a little more interested, now. "You not baby," I told him.

"Before was."

"No more."

Auntie was putting some dishes into the cupboard behind us and said, "You the smallest one?"

"Yes," he said, pointing at the fruit.

Auntie nudged my shoulder away from William's and squeezed between us on the bench. Her hand waved back and forth across the two circles of lychee before stopping above one group. She hesitated before lifting the smallest lychee.

"Me," William said.

"Yes. Mommy know."

What was it about Auntie's voice? Her words breathed where no breath belonged. Her shoulders slumped even with ours. And then she looked from one group of lychee to the other— from one "family" to the other.

"Before days," she said, shaking her head, "not same like this."

She lifted the tiny lychee from its pile and set it with the other pile. Then she turned toward her son. I could see the back of her neck as she tilted down toward his face. "Son," she told him, "you born Spencer's family."

I tried to see William but Auntie's head was in my way. She was telling him that he had been born to my family, that at first my parents were his.

"How I came this family?" he asked.

"Auntie Mariko bring you to me," she told him.

He held a hand over each of his ears and said, "I no can remember."

Gently, Auntie lifted the hands away from her son's ears. "Only one small baby, she said. "Just born. Only one week old you came."

I got the idea to lean backward and managed to see William from behind Auntie's back. He looked confused, unsure of what he had heard. Then I didn't notice him any longer because the hand on his back attracted me; around and around it rubbed, more desperate now, faster and faster, the mother rubbing the son.

"No need feel sad," she was telling him. "Today same like yesterday."

Uncertainty softened William's voice. "You still going be my mom?" he asked her.

Auntie hugged him, the same as she had when he was a

scared infant on her lap. Her arms encircled completely her only child and together they rocked. They rocked deep and deeper still, and at the end they rocked slowly, barely perceptible.

"Mommy and Daddy always take care you," she said, lifting his chin with her fingers. "But, son, every time need respect Auntie and Uncle. They bring you to me."

I felt uncomfortable, as if I'd overheard something private. There it was, all in the open. I wasn't sure where I should lay my hands, and I wasn't sure where I should aim my eyes, so I directed them all toward the bowl of lychee. But Auntie's hand rubbed my back, and when I looked at her, she smiled. She left the table, then. William and I scooted toward each other to fill the gap. Finally, now, after all these years I could talk to him about his birth.

"Before days you my brother," I said.

"The same like Taizo?"

"No. One little brother."

"Oh." He seemed puzzled and laid his head sideward on the table. I, too, laid mine on the table. As earlier, we faced each other from a sideward angle, but this time William appeared more tired. His fatigue showed in the heavy lay of his head. So we didn't talk further but I smiled, waited a while, smiled again, and this time William smiled back. Then I wondered if he was smiling at my crooked smile. But I just left it at that and felt tender toward my small cousin.

Taizo continued to separate his life from mine. He played with me reluctantly, as if placating a younger sibling was a duty of a firstborn son. I left fourth grade and entered fifth without the reassurance of my brother's friendship.

He became my father's ally. The two of them hurled directions at me, and their impassive faces couldn't hide the disappointments they realized over my inability to follow the logic of our ancestors.

We stood in the neighborhood market and waited for our turn at the cash drawer. The head of cabbage I was given to hold felt clammy against my hands. I wondered when my father would claim his turn to pay for our groceries.

"I think our turn now," I said quietly to my father.

"Stay back," he ordered. "Not turn yet."

I backed up against the side wall beside Taizo and watched as Mrs. Osaka hobbled to the drawer with her daikon, a long white radish that extended past her shoulder. I knew we had been waiting longer than she had.

"Was here first," I whispered to Taizo.

"She older. Quiet already."

I shifted the cabbage from one hand to another until I carelessly dropped it. My father glared as I retrieved it from the floor. From the opposite wall of the tiny store, Mrs. Nakasato called to my father, "You next."

"No," my father said, shaking his head. "Stay your turn."

"No, you," she insisted.

"You," he firmly said.

"Sure?" she asked.

He nodded.

Mrs. Nakasato, the elder of the two adults, acquiesced and stepped to the cash drawer. I glanced around to see who else was waiting to buy groceries and felt grateful that no additional customers were waiting.

Just then, Mrs. Lucas, a young mother from Filipino Camp, stepped from the produce bins and looked gingerly at my father. He indicated with his hand for her to step forward.

She nodded gratefully. "Little bit hurry," she said.

"You go," he confirmed.

"No mind?"

"No, no. You go."

Mrs. Lucas rushed to the cash drawer with her handful of long, dangling green beans. My father leaned near Taizo and said, "Must be some hurry."

Taizo nodded, unperturbed by the delay. I fidgeted, and with one slippered foot I scratched the opposite ankle. I held tightly onto the cabbage, though, remembering my father's glare.

"Taizo," I whispered. "How we ever going get up front?"

"No need worry. More better wait turn."

I glanced around the tiny store, wondering who else would appear with groceries, and determined that we were now the only shoppers in the market. The owner turned from her cash drawer and nodded toward my father. Only then did he step forward.

On the walk home I asked my father, "But what if more crowded? How we going get turn?"

My father didn't immediately answer. He seemed to consider my question, which I hadn't realized carried the weight he inferred. Finally, he answered. "When belong up front, somebody going put you there."

Maybe, I thought . . . maybe. I looked at Taizo and noticed he was nodding, storing my father's explanation as one more fact.

As we neared our home, we began to pass sugar workers returning from the day shift. "You going get away," my father reminded Taizo and me when a group of workers headed toward us. He had been telling us this for as long as I could remember. "Not going work sugar."

The men approached, and I studied them once again to confirm what I would never become. I'd never have to dress for the cane fields. The sugar workers wore layered clothing that protected them from the elements and insects. Boots overlapped pants, gloves overlapped long sleeves. I knew from my father that even the layers couldn't deter the most persistent centipedes and scorpions. Dad suffered with swollen ankles and wrists. One time, as he unwrapped his layered belt at the end of a shift, a centipede slithered into his pants at the waist. A field worker had to be alert and guard all his openings.

My father and the workers nodded and grunted in acknowledgment as the group passed us. The tired workers held their metal lunch cans limply, without swing. According to my father's plans for Taizo and me, we'd never carry metal lunch cans or wear layered clothing. We wouldn't curse the summer sun or the winter rain. My brother and I would never set cane on fire.

I looked toward the sky above the mill. The smoke drew the shape of a tornado above the smoke stacks, a wide oval that funneled narrowly at the stacks. Maui's customary trade winds were silent. Those winds would return to whisk away the smoke, but on this windless day, the smoke could form patterns above our valley.

We turned up Row Three. Mr. Sato, our across-the-street neighbor, walked toward home down the middle of the road while a car trailed him. He neither moved aside nor acknowledged the car. I doubt he even considered it.

"Try look," Taizo said as we reached our yard. "Uncle stay at our house."

Uncle Toshi nodded toward us from our front porch and held a beer in the air toward Dad. "Hurry," he playfully called to my father. "Some long I been waiting for drink my beer."

"Why never start?" my father said, walking more quickly now.

"What," Uncle said, "bring beer and never wait?" He shifted his eyes toward Taizo and me and said, as if confiding, "Not too polite, that."

Dad set the bag of groceries in the grass and took the beer from Uncle's hand. They sat together on the top step where Dad took a long drink. "You polite?" he said to my uncle. "Since when worry polite?"

"Quiet, you. Pretty soon I going take all my beer home."

My father smiled. Taizo and I settled on the lower steps. There, looking up, I watched my father form his lips to the shape of the bottle and swig the Lucky Lager beer.

Uncle opened two more beers and said, "Get not-so-good news."

"What," my father said, accepting the bottle.

"Going get strike."

"Only talk, that," my father told him. "Still early."

"Going get, I telling you," said Uncle, leaning his face toward my father's.

Dad took a drink and looked away. "Need for teach plantation one lesson," he said.

"Every time bring supervisors from mainland," Uncle agreed. "Never know nothing, them. No can even use machines."

"Us no look good in Supervisors Row," my father said.

Uncle nodded. "Going get strike. I telling you, going get."

Dad shrugged. "Then get," he said.

"What if kick us out the house?" asked Uncle, his eyebrows lifting high.

My father shook his head once, dismissing the idea, and took a thoughtful drink. "Not going kick out. Need us for harvest cane when strike pau."

"What about rice?" my uncle said. "What if no more rice? If get strike, rice bag come empty. If no more rice, house come empty."

"Can happen," my father said.

"Union get plenty rice bags, but what if no more enough?" asked Uncle. "Need plenty rice."

"What if?" my father said. "Maybe no more rice."

Uncle sighed. "Everybody going come wild if no more rice. Need rice."

My father repeatedly pounded the base of the emptied bottle into the palm of his opposite hand, then paused. "One empty rice bag more better than one empty man," he said.

Uncle shook his head. "Dumb Haoles. Only stupid, the new supervisor from the mainland."

"His boy in Spencer's class," my father said, looking down the steps toward me.

I drew back, momentarily unsettled that the conversation had turned to me. "Tom?" I asked, picturing the nice boy with the light blue eyes who had just enrolled in my classroom. He was the only Haole boy in my class.

"That one," confirmed my father. "His dad the one only yell every time."

"Tom nice," I said.

"Stay away him," my father warned. "Boys not equal if fathers not equal."

Unlike Taizo, I was not in the habit of believing everything my father said. I soon befriended the boy in my class, careful to keep the friendship within the confines of school. He let me call him, "Tom, Tom, the Piper's Son." His hair was the brown color of a sun-dried coconut, and what I thought, but didn't tell him, was that his rigid nose reminded me of Pinocchio's. My own face felt pliable compared to Tom's angles.

We played with marbles during recess. "Have you ever noticed that your marbles feel heavier than mine do?" Tom asked, using many words for a short idea.

"From Japan, these," I explained.

"These marbles are from Japan?" he eagerly asked, leaning forward. "Isn't that the place where the Japs live?"

I looked at Tom and realized from his open expression that he didn't understand the pain his question caused for me. How carelessly he threw out the word, "Japs," when the word caused my parents to shake their heads and shudder. Now Tom watched me, waiting. I picked up a marble, closed my hand around it, and tossed the marble around inside my fist. "Japanese live Japan," I answered.

"That's just what I said," he replied. "Is Japan somewhere around here?"

"Japan?" I said. "Hmmm." Japan had been a place I'd always heard about. Yet all I knew for certain was that it was someplace over the ocean. "Other side water," I said. "Japan stay other side water."

"When I rode on the ship to Hawaii," said Tom, mispronouncing the name Huh-why-yee, "I rode across the ocean. Maybe I passed Japan. I could have gone right by without noticing."

"Makes sense," I agreed.

He grabbed me, and we wrestled on the schoolyard grass. We rolled over and over, holding each other tightly. I ended up beneath Tom, looking up at his angular face. Those angles didn't frighten me because I knew the soft boy underneath.

Although I was secure in our equal worth, I did envy Tom's ocean crossing. My only concern about our friendship was that my father didn't think Haoles were worth knowing. I figured they didn't become worthless until they grew up. Tom and I had a lot of time until then.

As weeks passed, I became more daring. Our friendship ventured past the schoolyard grass. I followed Tom home to Supervisors Row and walked boldly through his front door, so much larger than my own. I had passed these homes many times and wondered what lay inside. Now I knew it was boys like Tom.

On the day I received an invitation to Tom's birthday party, I felt hopeful. I ran home and handed it to my mother, watching carefully for her initial reaction. Her eyes narrowed, and she shook her head.

"Cannot go?" I asked.

"Not sure," she said. "We need for ask Daddy."

"But he going say no," I reminded her. "No need even tell him."

"How can not tell?" she said. "Just try ask him. Maybe he going say yes."

I hoped against reason as I approached my father on the porch that afternoon. He sat with Uncle Toshi, and their conversation paused while Dad pulled the invitation from its envelope. "What this?" he said, reading.

"Tom having one birthday party."

"I told you stay away him."

"Everybody going," I said. "Marc Yamada's dad said yes."

"Who everybody? Not you."

"Going get ice cream," I quietly added.

Uncle Toshi reached over and tapped my father on the knee. "Let the boy go, Hiroshi. Only one birthday party."

"More than one birthday party," Dad said.

"Not," said Uncle. "Maybe that boy going grow up to be one

good Haole. Get good Haoles, you know. I met plenty in the war."

"No, he not going," my father said.

"Please, Dad?" I asked.

"I said not going," he scolded. "Enough already."

I took back the invitation and headed inside. For me there would be no birthday party and, more important, no chance to go all the way into friendship with a Haole boy. Later that evening, I lay in bed and overheard my parents discussing the party.

"Need for send gift," my mother said. "Somebody else can take for Spencer."

"No *need* send nothing," said Dad.

"Get invitation," my mother insisted. "Not polite if we no send one gift."

"Then send," said Dad.

"One dollar would be polite."

"Fine, one dollar then."

I have not forgotten the day of the party. Marc stopped by to pick up my gift envelope for Tom. I had lied to everyone about my reason for not going, claiming a conflict in plans.

"Too bad you busy today," said Marc, accepting the envelope. "No feel bad, but. Only a birthday party."

"More than one birthday party," I said bitterly, remembering my father's words.

Marc left for the party, leaving me alone on my back steps to think. The big issues of prejudice and power crossed my mind, a confusing surge of ideas, but I spent most of that afternoon thinking about the simpler issue of ice cream.

On the Wednesday afternoon of the next week, Tom followed me home from school. I didn't know how to tell him he couldn't come. I kept waiting for the chance to explain, but instead I found myself laughing when he tackled me in my front yard. My father was working that afternoon, but I knew he'd eventually find out. Haole boys didn't often play in the yards of Japanese Camp. We lay in my yard on our backs and watched as a group of screaming mynah birds gathered above us. Their wings flapped quickly. The birds all faced the same direction, as if in prearranged formation.

Tom rolled over on his side. "I think I know what the birds are yacking about," he said, pointing at the neighbor's hedge. "They spotted that mangey yellow cat."

I sat up and studied the cat. The animal was clearly discarded and wild. Its wet fur clung to a pitiful, ribbed body. The cat glanced at the commotion above. He then looked toward Tom and me, but dismissed us with obvious disdain. Tom stood and took a step toward him. The cat clawed at the air, daring the boy. Tom backed off.

Above us, the birds continued to scream. The cat stopped glancing upward and studied intently the croton hedge. Now, the birds became frantic. They saw the future that I couldn't. All the cat's instincts honed toward the hedge.

The cat jumped and plunged his front paws into the

branches. He turned toward Tom and me without fear, and from his mouth dangled a little bird, a miniature of those above. From the sky that bird's caretakers clattered and shrieked. The cat ran from their anger, and the group of birds flew silently away.

"That bird didn't have a chance in the whole wide world," said Tom.

"No more chance," I agreed.

We stood, shaking our heads at what we had seen, when Taizo came down the front walk holding his schoolbooks. He seemed momentarily confused over Tom's presence in our front yard, actually stopping in mid-stride to take in the scene. I forced a quick smile at my brother. I'm certain that he could sense my fear of getting caught with a Haole boy I was supposed to avoid. I watched Taizo's face carefully, the downward pull at the corners of his lips, waiting for him to smile in return. A fake smile would have been enough. Instead he strode past us with his mouth turned down.

Tom looked at me, perplexed, and that's when I told him we couldn't be friends any longer. Our friendship had become too close, had gone too far.

He listened, stunned. "Will they still let you play with me in school?" he asked.

"Can," I said. "No tell, but."

He started backing away down my front walk. "I guess I'll be seeing you tomorrow then," he said.

I nodded, watching the only blue-eyed boy I'd ever truly known walk away. "'Bye, Tom," I shouted. "'Bye." To myself I softly added, "Tom, Tom, the piper's son." I watched him walk backward all the way down our row. "Turn around," I shouted. "Turn around." He shook his head, refusing, his eyes locked on mine. Finally I could no longer distinguish the features of his face. I don't know how long I would have stood there, thinking about men, boys, and the years between, if Taizo hadn't come outside and taken hold of my elbow.

"We go," he said.

"Where going?" I asked.

"Just going," said Taizo.

I nodded, grateful to be going anywhere with him. We walked out of the rows and down the cane road. My thoughts turned away from Tom. I felt peacefully surrounded by the color green. Cane leaves flapped upon the stalks in the wind. I left Taizo behind and ran down the road with my eyes open, blurring my vision to cane green. As I ran down that cane road, head now held toward the sky, I assumed the color blue was as endless as the sky and ocean that surrounded our island. Green was a finite color, capable of being measured in rows.

I slowed and turned back up the road to meet Taizo. The sun felt hot on my face. My tongue ran across my lips, lingering in the corners. I imagined myself licking the taste of mango from the crevices. As I met up with Taizo, I told him I wanted to eat mango.

"Mango?" he asked. "Where get mango now?"

"Maybe the store tree," I said.

He shook his head. "All gone already."

"The Chinese Camp tree," I said.

"No more there. Only good, that mango. Everybody like take."

"I know where still get mango," I said, thinking. "Mr. Okamoto get mango."

"He no share," said Taizo.

I looked side-eyed at my brother. "Can just take. No need ask him," I said.

He became exasperated, leaning forward and clasping his hands behind his neck. "How can take? No can even *step* his backyard."

"Can be careful," I said.

Taizo shook his head. "Sneaky, you. Even bring one Haole boy our house. Get caught, right? You think not going get caught?"

"You same like Dad," I said, jutting my chin. "Before days more better. Go home already. I going get my own mango."

"What if caught?"

"Not going get caught. Only scared, you. Some good the mango going taste."

I began walking quickly toward Row One in a startling break-away from my brother's control. I hurried, determined, and became angry when I heard Taizo running to catch up with me.

He wasn't going to stop me this time. I whirled, facing him. "Now what?" I demanded.

"I coming," said Taizo, walking past me before I could get my feelings sorted. He continued walking while I remained rooted, confused over his abrupt change of mind. I shook my head in an emotional shudder, then ran to catch up.

We headed together toward the mango tree guarded by Mr. Okamoto, the man who yearly promised the neighborhood ladies that he would give them pickled mango. Later, when an auntie would rudely inquire about the pickled mango, he'd say, "Too bad I never made any this year. If had, I give plenty."

I glanced at Taizo as we walked and tried to get an idea of what had caused him to change his mind. Whatever it was, it wasn't visible. His face was as unreadable as ever, as if he were walking to an ordinary day of school or play. He didn't slow down until we reached the hibiscus boundary of Mr. Okamoto's backyard. There, he knelt behind the bushes and grabbed my arm. "Get down," he said, yanking me to my knees.

"Cannot see," I protested, knowing that if I stood I could easily see past the neatly manicured bushes.

"Look through branches."

I searched the hibiscus until I found a crack of light and pressed my face against the scratchy branches. The opening was only wide enough for one eye. I looked first with my right eye, then shifted to my left, then my right again. It wasn't satisfactory and reminded me of the yearly eye tests we were given in school, when we had to cover one eye. My eyes preferred to work in tandem. Then I discovered that by tilting my head sideways, I could look with both eyes through the vertical crack.

"He not there," I said to Taizo.

"Quiet."

I whispered loudly, "He not there."

"Back door stay open," whispered Taizo. "Maybe coming back."

"Can hurry," I said, still looking through the branches. "Can run fast."

"Need one lookout," said Taizo.

I turned toward him. "Lookout?"

"For warn in case he come outside."

"What the signal?" I asked.

Taizo pulled a ginger bud from his pocket and pulled off a layer. "You get the mango," he said. "If hear me whistle, come back already."

I nodded. "Go now?" I asked.

"Now," Taizo said, folding the leaf in half. "Careful."

I crawled to the end of the hibiscus row, confirmed with a quick glance that the yard was unguarded, and sprinted for the mango tree. Five mangoes dangled from a low branch. They smelled ripe, and I could see the juicy sap that ran down their bright red skins. They would suffice, though Taizo and I preferred to eat our mangoes half-ripe.

I stepped back and studied the tree for less-mature mangoes.

Some crunchy green mangoes hung about halfway up the tree. I was figuring out how best to reach them when I heard Taizo whistle. Alarmed, I looked around and spotted Mr. Okamoto on his back porch. I'd have to hurry. With one last look at the perfect half-ripe mangoes, I yanked the five ripe fruits from their stems and dropped them into my outstretched shirt. Then I dropped to the ground and crawled with one hand from the yard. My other hand cradled the mangoes trapped inside my shirt.

"Hey, boy. Who that!"

I froze upon hearing Mr. Okamoto's voice, afraid to look back toward him.

"You think I never see you?" he demanded. I turned and watched him run toward me, arms flailing. "What you doing my yard?"

"Nothing," I said.

"Crawl like one bug and never do nothing? Sit up," he ordered.

I obeyed, still holding the mangoes inside my rolled shirt.

"What get inside your shirt? Open it."

I let go of my shirt. The mangoes fell to the ground.

"Steal my mango! Going be sorry, boy. How many you take?" He came closer. His slippers pushed my legs aside as he counted the fruit on the ground. "Five. Greedy, you. Only one boy and take five mango."

I watched his feet. I thought certain he was going to step on me as he yelled above my head.

"Go already. Get out here and no come back."

I stood, ready to run, when I saw Taizo come around the end of the hibiscus and head toward me. "Come, Spencer," he said.

Mr. Okamoto nodded sarcastically. "So, never came alone for steal. Not surprised. You Fujii boys both same. I going tell your father. Some mad going be."

Taizo put his arm around my shoulder and began to lead me away. "No worry," he said.

Mr. Okamoto must have heard. "Better worry," he shouted. "Some trouble you going be."

I looked back over my shoulder at him. The tree stood menacingly behind him. He held a mango in each hand and shook his arms toward me. I shivered.

"No look," said Taizo. "No even look."

"He going tell Dad," I said.

"He will," agreed Taizo.

"What can happen?" I asked as we cut across to our row.

"No worry," he said.

"Maybe he not going tell."

"He will."

"What Dad going do?"

Taizo shook his head.

"Only my fault," I said. "I wanted for eat mango."

"Quiet. No say nothing."

"Was my fault, but."

"I went," said Taizo.

"You never wanted for go," I reminded him.

"Quiet already."

That afternoon Dad walked into the house without taking off his workboots. Taizo and I paused in our card game. Mom looked up from the pants she was hemming and stared at my father's boots. "Hiroshi?" she asked, puzzled.

My father didn't look at her. He stared only at Taizo. "Drop the cards," he demanded.

Our cards fell to the floor.

"Stand up."

We quickly obeyed. Taizo allowed me to stand close as we faced my father.

"What?" my mother said. "Something wrong?"

"Get thief in family," my father said, still focusing on Taizo.

Mother set aside her sewing and stood. "Thief?" she said. "Who thief?"

"Your boy steal."

Mom's face tightened. "Steal?" she said.

"Nobu meet me when work pau. Said the boy went steal his mango."

I huddled in the curve of Taizo's side. He stood tall whereas I crouched with fear.

"What for?" my mother asked Taizo, puzzled. "What for steal?"

"Son," interrupted my father. I looked, but his glare was concentrated only at Taizo. "What kind oldest son you?" he said.

Taizo, understanding that my father wanted no answer, said nothing. I tilted my head against his shirt and looked up toward my brother's face. I had thought that he was motionless, but now I noticed that his cheeks shook. There was a sway where I had thought only stillness.

My father spat his next words at Taizo. "You shame this family." He abruptly turned and left out the front door. Taizo had been granted words. I, nothing.

In the silence of the next few days, my father completed his discipline. Taizo changed after that day, and in our family that was the way to show you had learned. Taizo's solemnity acquired a new level. We never again stole mango, but that was the obvious resolution.

Taizo and I talked about Dad's reaction as we lay in bed the night of the theft. I said, "Sorry, Taizo."

"Nothing for be sorry."

"I only wanted mango. If never like, you not going be there."

"I went," said Taizo.

I almost responded, but instead I lay silent and tried to understand. Taizo had been there. That was all that had mattered to Dad.

I listened as Taizo's breathing eased into a rhythmic pattern that I recognized. The wind blew through our open window and crossed the sleeping boy to me. The wind drifted, floated, and I knew that outside the sugar cane shivered slightly. It was reassuring to know that the cane swayed gently, predictably, despite this tumultuous day.

My stomach churned, and I wondered how Taizo could so easily sleep. My feet kicked away the blanket. In order to understand my thoughts, I needed to talk. I rolled over and shook Taizo awake.

"Stop," he complained.

"Wake up," I said.

He pushed me away and I pushed back, angering him so strongly that he threw me from the bed. I got up and dove on him, punching at his stomach and receiving a blow across my ear. We rolled to the hard wooden floor, and he pinned my arms with his knee. He punched me in the stomach until I thought I couldn't breathe.

Taizo left me there, huddled, spent, trying to catch my breath, and he climbed back into bed. For some reason I thought he'd ask me if I was okay. I stayed on the floor a long time after I recovered, waiting.

FOR

THE

UNION

It occurred to me as I studied my dinner that the union would likely strike. The possibility that had been talked about for weeks had now shifted to probability. I picked through my cooked cabbage to find only three stringy slivers of Spam, whereas normally I uncovered as many as ten. "Going strike?" I asked, looking from one parent to the other.

My mother was seated next to me. "Not for boys to worry," she said, her chopsticks poised above her plate.

Dad nodded at her from across the table as his chopsticks carried a thin piece of aku sashimi to his lips. There, his hand paused while he said to me, "Just eat."

I looked at Taizo as I took a drink of milk and realized from his resigned face that he knew more than I. "Already on strike?" I asked, carefully setting down the glass of milk.

Taizo leaned slightly forward, as if to speak, then quickly straightened. He shook his head dismissively at me, his lips now tightly shut.

My father lifted his rice bowl toward his face, eyeing me past its rim. "Tonight," he told me.

I lay my fork beside my plate. "Then still get chance," I said hopefully. "Can change mind."

Dad and Mom looked at each other straight on. The lines that began at the corners of my father's mouth were determined, dug in. My parents did something then that I thought very strange: they watched each other as they continued to eat. Their eyes locked in a private understanding. I felt oddly uncomfortable and wanted to jolt them apart.

Later that evening when Dad left for Union Hall, Mom walked with him to the porch. In a startling moment of affection, my father placed both hands on my mother's shoulders, facing her. Then he pivoted and walked straight down the steps. My mother crossed her arms and pressed each hand against a shoulder.

The men of Japanese Camp met on the road. They greeted each other loudly, with an edge of gaiety. They patted each other's backs and acted as if they were going to a party. From the porches, their wives, children, and elderly parents watched silently.

I was in bed when Dad returned late in the night. It had been impossible to sleep until I knew about the strike, although Taizo had managed to sleep. My mother tried to get specific information from my father, who spoke more loudly than usual. I recognized the effect of beer upon his voice.

"What if lose everything?" she asked him. "Need for take care the kids."

His voice was light, a dancing sway. "How can lose? Union going take care everything."

"What about scabs?" she persisted. "I heard Kazu not going strike."

"No can break us. Too strong, the union."

"What if run out rice before plantation gives in?" my mother asked. I had the feeling she was following him around the room, talking to his back.

"Rice?" he answered incredulously. "You like see rice? Go Union Hall." He began singing, ignoring my mother's next questions. She must have finally given up, because as I fell asleep, all I could hear was my father singing the ditty about "Ching, Chang, Chinaman sitting on a fence, trying to make a dollar out of fifty cents." It was his favorite song after a few beers; I knew it well.

The next morning, my father took Taizo and me to Union Hall before school. We stood in a line of schoolchildren to get a week's worth of lunch tokens. The hall was filled with men from the camps. I knew them all by row, if not by family name.

A man called out to the crowd, "Get one more shipment rice coming." In reply, the men cheered, roared.

"Going fill this hall with rice," another shouted. I had no reason to doubt him. An entire inner wall of the building had disappeared behind a layer of hundred-pound rice bags. They were piled so high, so tightly, that it seemed not even air could get in the way of our rice. Against the opposite wall, boxes of canned goods had been stacked to the ceiling.

Two Haole men I had never before seen were organizing groups of men to go fishing and hunting. Surprisingly, the union members clearly respected them. The two men wore ILWU buttons, which further confused me. I thought it was the Haoles we were supposed to be striking against.

Later I would learn that one of the men was a Democrat named John Burns, "Jack" to his friends. He was the first Haole man I ever heard my dad speak of without a tinge of sneer. In later years, sugar camps all over the Hawaiian islands would help to elect this man governor.

That first day of the strike in late October was followed by months of sugar workers holding firm against the plantation. I measured the calendar against the lunch tokens we were allotted. Out of fear rather than actual hunger, I made sure to eat my entire school lunch, including the mushy carrots in my beef stew. I tried not to breathe as I chewed the carrots, which made them more bearable.

The strike did not give sugar workers a chance to rest; instead, each man worked long hours for the union. My dad carried signs outside the plantation gate and spat at Kazu Inagaki's boots each time he crossed the line. Mr. Inagaki was the shame of Japanese Camp.

With groups of men, my father hunted and fished. The bounty was brought back to Union Hall, along with wild guavas and plums from the woods and seaweed from the shore, and everything was divided. Men climbed cliffs to scrape off the opihi; as the strike progressed, and the opihi became more scarce, the men had to climb the island's most dangerous cliffs. On lucky days we would get bamboo shoots or even some octopus for dinner. Other men worked huge common gardens in the vacant areas among the rows of our camps, growing tomatoes, peppers, bittermelons, peanuts, green beans, and lettuce. I think it was the peanuts that worried me most because I was familiar with their long growing cycle.

At school, Tom was the only student in my class without union lunch tokens. Children refused to play with him in the schoolyard. Inside the classroom, we pulled our desks slightly away from Tom's, just enough so that the Caucasian teacher wouldn't catch on, but Tom would. We drew a line at school that was nearly as firm as the line outside the plantation gate.

"Could you maybe play marbles with me?" Tom asked when he found me alone beneath one of the school's palm trees. "We can use mine, and I'll let you keep any of the marbles you win." His shoulders hunched in fear of my answer.

I shook my head and took pleasure in Tom's disappointment, the thin veil that quickly covered his eyes. "Maybe can play tomorrow," I said flippantly, turning toward the trunk of the tree, away from Tom. I didn't intend to be vicious, but neither did I want to play with him. In order to play with Tom, I'd have had to cross the schoolyard picket line.

My father received a small weekly paycheck from the union strike fund. On payday, the neighborhood store was crowded with the families of striking sugar workers. On one such payday I accompanied my mother to the store. She brought with her a small bucket in which to carry home fresh tofu, a food staple we could get only with money. As we walked to the back corner of the store, I noticed that Mrs. Inagaki walked behind us. Customers were openly staring at her. My mother ignored Mrs. Inagaki, concentrating instead on the blocks of tofu in a big wooden tub. She took a long time deciding the exact block of tofu she wanted to buy. The store owner lifted it from the tub and lowered it gently into our bucket.

"What you making for dinner?" asked Mrs. Inagaki, edging up beside us. Her hair was more curly than usual, a new permanent that was despised by the women of Japanese Camp.

Without even acknowledging Mrs. Inagaki, my mother hurried away with her bucket of tofu. I was left behind to face the woman, and remembered that she had asked about dinner. "Pork tofu," I said, guessing, then went to find my mother at the front of the store. We were waiting for our turn at the cash register when Mrs. Inagaki sidled up beside Mrs. Sato.

"Nice for see you," said Mrs. Inagaki.

Mrs. Sato sniffed with a turned-up nose and turned to my mother. "I think you next, Mariko."

"No, you," my mother told her.

Mrs. Sato was careful not to look at Mrs. Inagaki. "You, Mrs. Tom."

Mrs. Tom shook her head. "I never get anywhere for go."

Mrs. Inagaki spoke up. "Maybe I can go next. I need for get home quick."

The women ignored her. "You next, Mariko," Mrs. Sato insisted.

We stepped up to the cash register. As I watched my mother carefully count out the change to pay for her tofu, I realized that Mrs. Inagaki would be left standing until there was no other customer in the store. No one would tell Mrs. Inagaki to step forward. The ladies would make her push.

The atmosphere at home had become steadily more grim. My parents talked little because my father refused to discuss the strike. Each time my mother prodded him with questions, he reacted angrily. "What you like me do?" he demanded. She hurried off without even glancing toward my father, and I quickly followed.

The strike extended through Christmas, a holiday which meant little to me except for the box of fireworks that Uncle Toshi and Auntie Sachi gave Taizo and me every year. I remember foolishly hoping the long box would somehow appear on Christmas morning, though my mother had warned me to expect nothing. I kept hoping all the way until New Year's Eve, when Taizo and I sat out back, listening to the firecrackers popping in Supervisors Row. My friend Tom likely had fireworks. We bad-talked him, as if he were responsible for our disappointment.

The next day wasn't any better. We traditionally spent New Year's Day at our friends and neighbors, eating abundantly in each kitchen. Only my mother would remain home throughout the day, ready to serve anyone who stopped by our home. On the New Year's Day of the strike, we visited our friends as usual. No one mentioned the strike. Each auntie offered me food from her scant table, but my mother had sternly cautioned me to take as little as possible. I ate a lot of rice.

As we turned the page of the union calendar from January to February, I began to wonder whether the strike would ever end. On February 5th, it did. The union won after holding out for more than three months. The good news was shouted up and down the rows of Japanese Camp. My mother and I were watching Auntie hang clothes in her backyard when we learned the strike was over. Auntie threw a perfectly clean shirt in the air and let it fall to the dirty ground.

My dad and uncle did their celebrating at Union Hall, then continued later that evening on our front steps. "Come, boy," Dad said as I hesitantly stepped out the front door to watch. "Sit."

I slipped into the narrow space between the two men, careful not to bump the hands that held their beers.

"Where Taizo?" Dad asked.

"Sleeping," I said.

"You suppose to be sleeping, too," Dad said. "Never mind. Today can stay up." He leaned forward and looked past me. "For the union," he said, raising his beer across my body, toward Uncle.

Uncle met Dad's beer with his own. "For the union," he said, the bottles clinking in front of my face.

I leaned away from the bottles, the fragile glass. I sensed a recklessness that scared me and wished I hadn't sat between the men and their bottles.

Dad slung an arm behind me and tapped Uncle on the shoulder. His arm banged against my back. "So, anyway, what we won?" he asked him.

Uncle found that hilarious. He laughed uproariously; the beer sloshed from his bottle. "Who said we won?" he said, wiping beer from his knee. "Just never lose."

"The union never lose," Dad said.

"Yes," Uncle agreed, becoming more quiet, "at least never lose."

I felt trapped by the men and their emotions. I stood, but my father grabbed my arm and pulled me back down. "Where you going?" he said.

"Bed."

"Now tired? Thought you not tired."

Uncle reached over and touched Dad's knee. "Let the boy

go," he said. "Even us should go bed. Need for get up early tomorrow."

"No can be late for work," Dad said drunkenly.

"Besides," said Uncle, "I like see the looks on the supervisor's face."

Dad hurled his beer bottle toward the yard. It smashed against a plumeria branch and broke into pieces. He leaned across my thighs to face Uncle. "Throw your bottle," Dad told him.

"Still get beer inside," said Uncle, holding up the bottle so that Dad could see. "No can waste good beer." Uncle took a long drink, tilting the bottle upright. He tongued the last drops of beer from the rim. Then he hurled the bottle toward the tree, cracking a limb, and stood. "Bet you never thought I can hit the tree," he said to my dad.

My father then stood, leaving me down at the men's knees. He shook Uncle's hand above my head before reaching down with the same hand to tousle my hair. "Time for sleep, boy."

I quickly got out of there. As I fell asleep, I could still hear them outside. The last I heard they were drunkenly plotting Uncle's route home, determining how best he could travel between Rows Three and Four of Japanese Camp.

The union planned a victory celebration for the following weekend. Taizo and I let William join us early Saturday morning to check out the preparations at Union Hall. We stood outside for a while to watch a pig cook over a fire. It was skewered lengthwise, the pole stuck in one end and out the other. The animal's burning flesh smelled good.

We stepped inside the hall. Two men were tacking a banner that read "For the Union" against a wall. Others were arranging tables in rows. Mr. Sato spotted us and playfully stuck a broom in Taizo's hand. Quickly, Taizo handed it to William. William just as deftly passed it to me.

Mr. Sato laughed and took back his broom. "Better get away before somebody make you boys work."

The three of us took off running. We stopped by our homes for our slingshots and Taizo's BB gun before heading for the woods. If we got lucky, we'd get some birds.

Hours later, when the cooked pig was being shredded into pieces and rain poured into the valley, I came running back to Union Hall alone. The rain had chased everyone inside. I pushed open the door and found my father in a circle of men. His face immediately paled when he saw me.

"Need help," I shouted, slumping to the floor.

My father was shaking my shoulders. "What happen?" he pleaded.

"Taizo," I said, unwilling to look at him. "Taizo cannot get out of the reservoir."

We all began running.

DIVISIONS

Plantation workers tied ropes around Taizo's lifeless body and pulled him from the reservoir while my family and neighbors watched. The rain continued to fall. Someone wrapped Taizo in a quilt, and workers lay him on the back of a cane wagon for the ride home.

My mother's cries were lost in the sound of rain as she climbed into the wagon with him. One of her hands pressed against Taizo's body to soften the jolts of rutted fields. My father walked behind the wagon in steady, even gait. The rest of us followed silently.

William came up from behind me and put his hand in mine. He was still so young that he looked up at me and surprisingly grinned, perhaps hoping that I would reassure him with a smile.

When I couldn't, he refused to give up. His mouth further tightened into a grin that sickened me. I dropped his hand and shoved him away with my elbow. A few minutes later, his smile gone, he again took my hand.

That night, Taizo came home in his casket. He lay in the parlor near the altar. I could not look at him when the others were around and avoided the room in the hours that my mother wept over him. I crept to my brother only when alone. What surprised me most was how easily death had come, for until then I had assumed death was more than a childhood struggle. I pushed two of my favorite marbles between the second and third fingers of Taizo's overlapping hands, and they glittered. If my parents noticed, as surely they must have, they didn't remove the marbles. It was the first thing I checked for each time I stepped up to the casket.

People left flowers in our parlor and outside our front door. I pulled the bud from a ginger plant and took it to my room. That night I unwrapped a layer from the bud and made a whistle. I lay in bed and whistled carefully, quietly, remembering how recklessly my brother and I had whistled with our mouths toward the sky.

On the second evening, Taizo's casket was moved to the Buddhist church. My father and I sat on either side of the casket, waiting for plantation workers who could more conveniently visit at night. Hours passed and nobody came to view the body. The special visitation lights above us shone brightly. Black beetles fell from the hot lights onto Taizo's face and body. My father and I took turns picking them out.

Quietly we sat. I was grateful for the quiet because I feared the day that my father would question me about what had happened at the reservoir. In the sorrow of my brother's death, my parents hadn't yet turned on me. I feared the knowing look in my mother's eyes, and, even more, the angry words from my father. I didn't want to allow him even the slightest opening.

Two plantation workers visited after the 11 o'clock shift change. It took them a while to get their boots off at the door and come down the aisle. They nodded to my father, a perceptible bow to sorrow, and he thanked them for coming. I was not spoken to and did not speak.

Around midnight Uncle Toshi arrived to spend the rest of the night with my father. He handed each of us a plate of nishime and tofu. Our religion forbade the eating of animal flesh between death and cremation.

I ate and walked home, relieved to leave the somber church and go to sleep. My bedroom was still dark hours later when I awoke to the sounds of my mother preparing for the day of her oldest son's funeral. I lay in bed and listened to the echoes of drawers, pots, and cupboard doors. I smelled rice.

Unsure if it was night or morning, I walked toward the light in the kitchen. Mom's hipbones pressed her housedress against the table as she formed rice balls with her hands. I sat on the bench to watch.

"Go back sleep," she said wearily, pressing a handful of rice into a ball. "Still early."

I shook my head. "No can."

"Can rest, but." She added the rice ball to many others on a large platter.

"I like watch," I told her.

She shrugged and pulled her cooking pot closer. She picked up the salt container and sprinkled salt into the palms of her hands. With a wooden paddle she scooped rice into a small bowl. Then she turned over the bowl and the rice dropped into her salted hands. She cupped them together and pressed the rice into a firm ball.

"How come round?" I asked her. Their shape bothered me because our rice balls were usually triangular.

"Today eat round rice ball."

"Can make me one triangle?"

"No can."

"Why we never ate round before?"

"Did, when Grandpa die."

"Why not eat round on regular day, then?"

"Bad luck, that," my mother explained, scooping more rice into the small bowl.

She looked toward the hallway at the sound of the front door. My father walked heavily to the kitchen. I had never seen him walk so tentatively. She watched him, waiting for him to speak.

He lay his head against the kitchen wall. "Church ready," he said to her.

She nodded slowly. "The bath hot."

He pushed away from the wall. "Where my good clothes?" he asked.

She looked quickly away from him, as if there was something in his eyes she didn't want to see. "Stay washhouse already."

Dad left through the back door for his bath. I watched my mother make rice balls until he returned inside. Then I took my own furo bath. I washed quickly over the drain in the washhouse floor, rinsing with a bucket of water, and settled in the wooden tub with water to my neck. My mother had added wood and begun the fire unusually early that morning. The wood burned in a metal box at the far end of the tub, near my feet, and the fire crackled. My finest starched pants and shirt for my brother's service lay on the nearby stool.

After I returned inside, my mother bathed. She put on her funeral dress, and our family walked to the church. The neighbors did likewise. Houses emptied throughout the camps. The Sato family walked across the road from us. Mr. Sato walked barefoot. His good shoes dangled from his hands.

I recall the polished shoes lined up outside the church door, more shoes than I had ever seen. An uncle from Lahaina stood outside on the lawn with a hooded camera and took photographs of the mourners in their best clothes. People lined up for the chance.

When someone died from Japanese Camp, the women of the same row as the mourning family assisted with the preparations. The aunties of Row Three had been cooking, cleaning, and comforting my mother since Taizo's death. Now, two aunties sat outside the church at a card table to collect offerings called koden. They opened the plain white envelopes and carefully recorded in a little book the amounts given. Most families gave us three dollars, equal to nearly three hours of work in the cane fields, to help pay for Taizo's expenses.

My parents sat on either side of me in the front row of the church. Auntie, Uncle, and William filled the rest of the bench. I stuck out my foot and touched Taizo's casket with my toe. My mother reached down with her hand and pressed against my knee so I would stop.

I turned around and looked between my parents' shoulders as I waited for the service to begin. People continued to enter the church. They gathered along back walls and sat closely together on the church benches. Taizo's mourners came from all the different camps and Supervisors Row. I nodded when I saw Tom. He carefully lifted his hand and waved.

Candles and incense burned on the altar. Two vases of Auntie Sachi's carefully arranged orchids rested beside them. Pikake leis draped them all. Birds of paradise, red and yellow gingers, and carnations lay bundled at the foot of the altar stairs.

The service began with the ringing of a bell. It seemed as if the reverend had just begun talking when my mother signaled with a tug on my arm that the service was finished. Suddenly it was all over, and we were filing outside.

The men of Row Three carried the casket outside to the bottom of the church steps. I watched from the churchyard, worried that they would drop Taizo, until they carefully set him down. All my relatives lined up on either side of the casket except for the uncle with the camera. He was the only one who knew how to take the picture. I stood farthest from the casket, next to William. Somebody I didn't know stood behind us. He rested one hand on William's shoulder, the other on mine. My photographer uncle raised his arm and took the picture. A few weeks later he mailed us the long, narrow picture, which my mother rolled and added to the collection in her altar.

Only the six of us who were closest to Taizo attended his cremation the afternoon of the funeral. Dad, Mom, Uncle, Auntie, William, and I stood in a small room and looked at the body for the final time. Taizo had been dressed in a new gray suit with many pockets that an auntie in our row sewed for him. She said boys need lots of pockets.

As we looked at him, each of us broke down. My mother and auntie held each other. The rest of us stood alone. Dad was the last to cry. He sat on the floor, his back against Taizo's casket, and held his head with his hands. The tears were the only ones I saw him shed over his son's death. They flowed in a current of pain. I remember wishing the tropical rains could come into our tiny room and cover his wrenching cries, as rain had covered my mother's on the day of the drowning.

The undertaker knocked on the door of the small room and entered. Dad stood up. My mother gave the undertaker Taizo's urn. His name had been engraved in both English letters and Japanese calligraphy, even though neither Taizo nor either of my parents had ever been to Japan.

We returned home, never to see Taizo again. Aunties had prepared our house for a large gathering. I followed William into our yard and up the front walk. We had nearly reached the front steps when Dad tapped me from behind. "Come this side, boy," he said. He stepped from the dirt path to the grass.

William paused on the bottom step. "I can come, too?" he asked.

"No," my father answered.

William looked at me and shrugged. I stepped onto the grass and watched as he continued up the steps with the others and walked inside.

My father walked quickly around the side of the house, and I struggled to keep up. I was practically running as I followed him to the back side of the washhouse. He stopped, then, and looked at me. His shoulders pulled back. I knew he was going to talk about Taizo's death. His eyes flashed hatefully at me.

"Son," he demanded.

I looked at the ground. "Yes."

He spoke the next words in a careful, level tone. "Taizo never like water."

I shook my head. "No."

"Why he went inside?"

I shrugged, uncertain. "Wanted for go," I said.

"No make story, now."

I paused and consciously took quick breaths. "Not making story."

"No?" my father said. "Then why you say Taizo like go inside?"

"He went," I said, remembering Taizo giving me the same explanation the night we stole the mango.

Dad didn't respond, and I felt relieved. He wouldn't have the same conversation twice. Suddenly, abruptly, "Look me," he demanded. "You going lie over Taizo ashes?"

I looked at him, and the flash in my father's eyes knocked me back up against the wall of the washhouse. My hands tightened into fists at my mouth.

"No lie," he warned me.

"I not going lie," I said, and began to cry. My father was backing me up into the memory of the muddy water. My throat made tight, choking sounds.

"Pau already," my father ordered. "Not going ask. I know already. But no forget, boy. No lie."

I nodded.

"Stop crying."

I smeared the tears from my face with both hands. When my father was satisfied that I had erased the evidence of tears, we walked around to the front of the washhouse and up the back stairs. We pulled off our good shoes, and Dad pushed open the screen door.

People were crowded into the kitchen. Somehow, I maneuvered my way to the parlor. It was even more crowded there.

People sat on our furniture, some folding chairs, and our wooden floor. Others continued to arrive through the front door. I stood there, bewildered.

"Go eat," an auntie suggested.

Instead I went to my bedroom. I shut the door behind me and shoved the guests' sweaters to Taizo's side of the bed. I lay down to think, but, almost immediately, someone knocked. I pushed up to my elbows as the door slowly opened.

"Go eat," said Auntie Sachi, peeking through the opening.

"I coming soon," I told her.

"William stay eating already."

"I coming," I said again.

She stood at the door, waiting, until I reluctantly got up from the bed. "Can eat outside with William," she said as I passed her and stepped into the parlor.

There, I wound around the guests in an attempt to get down the hallway and into the kitchen. Many people were in my way, and I felt like pushing them aside. Instead I made fists in my pockets and waited for the guests to notice they were blocking my way.

"Oh, why you never tell me for move," someone would say, and I'd respond, "Not in my way." That person would move, but I'd get stuck again a few steps later.

When I was finally able to reach the kitchen, I stood looking at the table of food. There was so much food that I didn't know what to choose. The neighborhood ladies sensed my indecision and prepared a plate for me. "Give him that," one said, and,

"More better he eat this kind noodle," said another. On top of the food my mother added a rice ball. "No can forget rice," she said in a hoarse voice.

"Why your mother made rice?" Mrs. Sato said to me. "No need for her to cook. We get plenty rice."

I looked to my mother for the answer, and she shrugged. "No can have too much rice," she said.

I headed outside, carefully stepping into my slippers without tilting my plate, and found William sitting on the grass. He looked up and smiled as I approached. I sat across from him and balanced the plate on my thighs. He welcomed me, but said nothing. The day had been so full of voices that I was relieved when William didn't immediately talk.

He looked at me with those young eyes of his, eyes looking for help from somebody older. Only the two of us truly knew what had happened to Taizo. We should have listened to my older brother. Given one more chance, I would have. William and I had been there and would know the same regrets.

"Almost pau," I told him gently. "We going make it. Even the funeral stay over."

He scooted closer to me and touched his foot to mine.

"No worry," I said. It was what I wished someone would say to me.

"You think Taizo stay mad?" asked William.

I looked at my young cousin and considered his question. I wanted to tell him that Taizo hadn't been angry, but William would know that wasn't true. Taizo had been furious. I rubbed my toe against William's. "Never mind," I told him. "Never mind, already."

"Never mind?" he asked, puzzled.

"Cannot help," I said. "So never mind."

He nodded tentatively and continued eating. Once again I had told him what I needed to hear.

I paused with my chopsticks above my plate and looked at my food. The rice ball still bothered me. I had begun to sense that nothing would ever be the same now that Taizo had died, and the round rice ball confirmed it. With my hands cupped, I carefully pressed the ball into a triangle.

That was the main division in my life, the dividing moment. The funeral and the days before it were all part of Taizo's death. I changed the rice ball, and everything since has been after.

"Why you did that?" asked William, his eyes wide.

"I no like it round," I said.

"Oh. Can change mine?"

"Can." I picked up the rice ball from William's plate and made it into a triangle. "There," I told him, setting it into his hand. "No tell, now."

"I not going tell," he said.

I looked straight at him and my face tightened. "No tell nothing," I told him sharply.

He looked surprised and then thoughtful. I stared at him so that he'd understand I meant it. Fortunately, William depended upon me. "I not going tell nothing," he said.

WILLIAM

The oriental lettering on Taizo's headstone reminded me of the advanced chapters of my fifth-grade mathbook that our teacher ignored. I reached out to touch the flow and geometry of my brother's name, carefully following the Japanese outline. The tentativeness in the slow trail of my finger felt uncomfortable. With both hands I reached out more deliberately to cover Taizo's name, my fingers splayed like a Japanese fan. My hands pressed firmly against the etched characters, as if Taizo's name could be absorbed into the permanent lines of my hands.

Behind me, my family had almost finished their sunset picnic. Other families circled other graves. At the graves of our loved ones we had begun Obon, an annual Buddhist celebration to honor the dead. Tonight we would pray, dance, eat, and play. It was the second-best party of the year, after New Year's.

A spray of Auntie Sachi's orchids were propped up in an old mayonnaise jar as an offering upon the grave. Their delicate fragrance mixed with the unsettled smell of graveyard dirt. I closed my eyes, hands pressed against the stone, and remembered the day we buried my brother's empty casket. My mother referred to it as burying Taizo's last bed. It was an odd burial because the urn with Taizo's ashes had already been placed on a shelf of the church. Before the cremation, my mother had decided that the casket should not be burned, so it had been set aside, without a body, and two days later we buried it. I liked to believe that some of Taizo's coarse head hairs lay inside the casket, or, perhaps, the two marbles I had pressed between his unyielding fingers. It seemed likely that something had been left behind, now marked by the two languages of his carefully chiseled name.

William's knee brushed mine as he knelt beside me. He reached out and pulled my hands from the stone. I shook my hands free and, as earlier, traced the Japanese version of Taizo's name. As I traced, William's finger began to trail mine.

"No follow me," I ordered in a low voice that the adults behind us wouldn't hear.

William drew his hand away from the stone.

"Bad things happen if follow me," I whispered, referring to Taizo's death.

"Long time, already," said William, lifting his chin and eyes toward mine.

"Not even one year."

"I scared I might tell what happen."

I looked back over my shoulder and made sure the adults weren't listening. "No can tell," I reminded him. "No can ever tell."

"Cannot help if I tell on accident."

I glared at him. "No talk like that."

William glared back equally. "I say what I like say," he said.

I tried unsuccessfully to stare him down. We both concentrated all thought into those stares so that neither of us even breathed. But then his eyes softened, and mine, until we were just two boys breathing regularly again.

The adults talked happily behind me, laughing, chiding, as if this were any picnic at any park. With a barely perceptible nod of my head, I let William know I was returning to the others. He nodded in the same manner and followed.

We sat nearest the women, who had finished eating and were now waiting for the men to finish. All four adults wore their traditional Japanese kimonos. The men's kimonos were serious browns, beige, and black. The women wore the bright colors of flowers and autumn leaves. Their decorative golden threads flickered in the weakening sun.

Auntie Sachi, both hands upon her head, was complaining about a few hairs turning gray. "Must be getting some old," she was saying.

Dad flicked his chopsticks dismissively. "You old? If you old, what me? Ancient?"

"I think so," Auntie said, pointing. "You ancient."

Dad smiled and bit into his namasu. Mom giggled with the proper restraint of her kimono, covering the giggle with cupped hands. Auntie didn't care as much about tradition and laughed loudly.

"Better not laugh," Uncle teased his wife. "Hiroshi look only good in his samurai clothes. You going look that good in few more years?"

"Course," Auntie said, nose in the air. "Some good I going look."

Uncle studied her face and grinned. "Not so sure," he said. "More better we wait and see."

Auntie feigned hurt feelings. "If you not sure already, no more rice for you."

"What?" Uncle asked, eyebrows high. "Not going cook rice?"

"Going cook," Auntie answered smugly. "Just none for you."

Uncle clutched his stomach as if the air had been knocked from him. "Remind me when I stay army. Bad memory, that. Hawaii guys came some tired for eat potato." He took hold of Auntie's arm and added, "I miss my rice same like I miss my Sachi."

Auntie playfully pushed away Uncle's arm. "You only miss me same like rice?"

"Hey, that's plenty, you," Uncle teased, rubbing the arm as if she had actually hurt him. "Not everybody gets miss same like rice."

Dad nodded toward Auntie. "You on same level as rice," he told her. "No can complain about that."

Auntie shook her head, unconvinced. "You lucky tonight Obon," she said to Uncle. "I stay in good mood. Besides, the music start already. Almost time for go."

She and my mother began to clean up the picnic. The only plate left undisturbed was Taizo's, which lay upon his grave. My mother opened a paper bag and pulled out a mango, which she handed to me. To William she handed an orange.

We lay the fruit as an offering upon the grave. My mother and auntie came up behind us and knelt while the men stood. We remained quiet as the minutes passed. I listened to the conversations at other graves until my father announced, "Time for go next door."

William looked up. "Can go now?" he confirmed. "Can go Bon dance?"

Auntie reprimanded him sharply. "Obon," she scolded, emphasizing the respectful prefix. The other word for which our family routinely used the same prefix was ohashi, the Japanese word for chopsticks.

"Obon," William repeated.

My father nodded. "Time for go." He reached into his pocket and gave William and me a dollar each. Uncle did the same. "No make trouble," Dad told us.

"At Obon dance?" said Auntie, straightening the obi belt of her kimono. "How can make trouble at Obon?"

Less than one hour later, William and I lay with our stomachs pressed against the roof of the church. From that position we could see most of the churchyard below. Nearly all the residents of Wainoa had come to celebrate; hundreds and hundreds of people filled the yard. The smells that wafted up to the roof were sweet, those of incense and cooked teriyaki. As William and I watched, ladies from our camp took turns singing Japanese songs for those who danced in organized circles around a huge drum. The dull pounding of the drum vibrated in my stomach, as if the whole world were being shaken.

William and I had come prepared. Our water guns were full. As planned, we concentrated our attention on the four rings of dancers. They circled the drum like the concentric waves that form when a rock is tossed in calm water. My mother and auntie were following behind Mrs. Sato, who led the second ring. Among the dancers, I spotted most of the girls from Japanese Camp and a few of the boys.

"Who you going shoot?" William asked.

"Get plenty girls for pick from," I answered. "Need for shoot somebody who not going complain."

"Can practice on lantern," said William. He rolled over on his back and I did the same. Above us, paper lanterns criss-crossed the churchyard on carefully strung wire. Hundreds of the decorative lanterns, lit with reflected light, rocked in the mild trade winds. William shot at a lantern, jolting it.

"Good, that squirt gun," I noted. "Plenty power."

We rolled back onto our stomachs to choose our victims. I decided to try for Helen Goto. She was so quiet that I doubted she'd make a squeak. Just then she disappeared around the far side of the huge drum. I decided to get her on her next trip around.

When I aimed, I aimed for her kimono. She wiped her cheek, however, looking suspiciously at the sky.

"Good one," William complimented.

"She think was one bird," I said. My eyes scanned the dancers to select my next target. I settled on Michi Kato, one of my favorite girls. She lived only a few houses away in Row Three, and never chided me for being two years younger than she. Unfortunately, she was dancing in the innermost circle. My aim needed to be accurate.

"Got her!" William suddenly pronounced.

"Who you shot?" I asked, scanning the dancers for evidence.

"Look Sandy in outside circle. Only good I got her."

Sandy was clearly out of step. As the other dancers pulled their right arms in, Sandy stuck hers out. "You got her, for sure," I told William. "No can even dance right."

He lay on his back and laughed, holding his stomach.

"Careful, you," I said. "Somebody going hear."

"Who going hear?" asked a familiar voice as Uncle Toshi

climbed over the side of the building to our roof. He looked comical, hoisting his kimono high.

I was relieved it was Uncle instead of Dad. "Just having fun," I said.

"Not causing trouble," William added.

Then Uncle noticed our water guns and started laughing. "Naughty, you boys. How your aim?"

"Not bad," I said, somewhat relaxing. I still wasn't sure how much trouble we might be in. "Got Helen Goto good."

"What about you, boy?" he asked his son.

"I shoot Sandy," he said.

"Masa's girl?" Uncle asked, smiling.

William nodded. "All crooked her dancing came."

"What if the ladies catch you?" Uncle asked.

I looked at William and we both shrugged.

"See," Uncle said, more stern now. "More better you boys think. Give me the water gun."

We handed our water guns to him and watched, amazed, as Uncle lay carefully on his stomach, one water gun in each hand.

"What you going do?" William asked him.

"Shoot Mom," he said.

William and I inched ourselves toward the edge of the roof and watched as Uncle squirted his wife. Auntie brushed at the back of her neck, careful not to lose her step. William grinned until the grin became rubbery, and he burst out laughing. I couldn't help it and laughed, too.

We might not have got caught because two laughing boys aren't complete cause for attention. Then Uncle began laughing. William and I quieted, watching his belly shake as he lay on his back, but then we started up again. By the time we finally all stopped laughing and looked back down at the dancers, Auntie was looking right back at us with knowing eyes.

Uncle waved. Auntie refused to wave back, but that didn't matter. I wasn't worried one bit.

"Cool up here," said Uncle, lying on his back. "Good view, too."

I lay next to Uncle. William scrambled to his opposite side and also lay. The lanterns were our stars.

"Nice, Obon," said Uncle, pillowing his head with his hands. "Good for laugh and have fun."

"I wish Taizo can be here," I said.

Uncle sighed and quietly said, "Maybe Taizo here."

It seemed so possible right then that I actually shifted my eyes to check. When I saw nothing but an empty stretch of roof, I willed him to my side, picturing him right there upon his back. I looked him in the face and was horrified to see the cruel way he looked back at me. His eyes accused me. It was so unexpected that I gasped.

Uncle shifted to his elbows. "What happen?" he asked.

"Nothing."

"You sure?" he asked.

I nodded, hugging myself at the waist. I felt like turning to

Taizo once more and asking him to explain. That's when, with a sudden clarity, I realized what was to be my greatest pain in the years to come. I could talk to Taizo all I wanted, but I had clearly seen something when I looked at his face. He didn't want me anywhere near him. He would answer no questions, accept no apologies. The distance between us was growing.

In the days and months to come, I began to back away from the memory of my older brother. Time passed in a blur of heavy winter rains. I grew to love the rains that had covered the sound of my mother's pain and looked forward each year to the rainy season. I imagined my unheard cries all mixed up with the rain, then evaporating.

I outgrew all the clothes Taizo once had worn. I also outgrew William and his grin. Our distance didn't seem a conscious choice on my part, but more of a natural instinct. I pretended not to miss him and never gave a thought as to whether he might have missed me. When William was around, I felt as if I had to turn and acknowledge all that was behind me. It was better with nothing but a future.

Then one afternoon I happened to be walking toward William on the cane road when I recognized that he was wearing Taizo's clothes. My mother had passed them down after me. I paused and stared.

The cane rows swayed on either side of him as he continued to walk steadily toward me. He had reached childhood's middle years, when the shoulders are comparatively wide, but thin. I realized, with a start, that William had had no choice in our distance. I had pulled away from him the same as Taizo had pulled away from me. I felt a physical shift, a settling in my head, and understood better, then, the backing away of brothers.

"Taizo's shirt, that," I said, pointing with my chin as we met on the road.

He shrugged and looked me in the eye. "Fits."

"Might as well wear it," I said.

He nodded. "No sense throw away."

I folded my arms and studied him. "How you been?" I asked.

"Same."

"I no see you much."

"Same," he repeated.

"Where you going?" I asked, wondering where he was headed that afternoon.

"Nowhere. You the one leaving."

"You heard?" I asked, surprised.

"Everybody know," said William.

My stomach tightened as I thought of my mom and dad. They must have heard from others by now that I wouldn't be attending college. To avoid facing their disappointment, I hadn't yet told them of my army enlistment.

"Mom said you going Vietnam," William said.

"Maybe. Main thing is to get away."

"What your parents think about you enlisting?"

"I never told them," I admitted.

"Look at you," said William. "Still one coward."

His snicker was maddening. "Why you talk like that?" I said.

He shook his head in a slow, superior way and said, "Never mind." He tried to walk past me, but I reached out and grabbed his arm. "Get off me," he warned.

"Just no talk like that."

"I talk how I like," said William, jerking his arm free. "You done telling me what to say."

I heard the hurt in his words and placed my arm around his shoulder. He half-heartedly tried to wriggle free before allowing my arm to settle.

"We can go store," I said. "Can buy soda."

"Nothing else to do," said William.

We walked together toward the little market to buy two bottles of soda. The cane stood taller than either of us, and that was how I wanted to remember it.

Up the road William and I walked, faces away from the water, the younger boy leaning against the older, the ocean quiet behind us, the mountains quiet before us, and the sugar cane around us, all around us, and taller than either of us would ever be.

PERSPECTIVE

When you start college?" my mother asked, pretending to know nothing about my army enlistment. She and my father were eating dinner across the table from me. Mom lifted a bottle of soy sauce and poured a careful amount of the liquid onto a tiny plate. "We been saving money for long time so you can go college," she added.

I glanced anxiously from my mother to my father, neither of whom would meet my eyes. "I going army," I said, my gaze settling on my mother's forehead. "They say I can be one military photographer."

"College more better," said Mom, her eyes concentrating on the tiny chili pepper she broke open and stirred into the circle of soy sauce. "The Kimura boy going mainland college."

I pressed the tines of my fork upon the table, determined I would not speak again until my mother met my eyes. After a long, quiet pause she glanced furtively at me, hoping, perhaps, to catch me unaware. I locked eyes before she could politely glance away.

"I already sign the papers," I said, dipping my chin to maintain eye contact. "I went for sign my name."

Dad reacted to this admission with words that rattled the tines of my fork against the table. "We save our money for what?" he demanded. Resolutely I faced him and his words. My shoulders were square with his as he continued. "I work in cane field so you can take picture?" he asked, his palms pressing the table. "You going end up working sugar. Look Uncle Toshi. He went army and what? Only came back for work sugar."

"I not planning to come back," I said, wondering even as I spoke where else I would go.

"One sugar worker," said Dad. "What I work for all these years?"

"Maybe can change mind," Mom offered, her voice lifting in a hopeful way.

"No," I explained, "stay legal already. I sign the paper."

"Tea and rice?" Mom asked, noticing I had nearly finished my meal.

I nodded, scooping rice into my bowl. She hurried around the table with the teapot and added tea to my rice bowl's brim. "I get until July 4th," I said, mixing the tea and rice with the long end of my fork. "Then I go."

"Where?" she asked, resettling across from me.

"California for basic training. New Jersey for photography school."

"After that?" she prodded.

I sipped some tea, straining the rice with my teeth. "Maybe Vietnam."

"Vietnam? You should go Japan instead."

"Japan?" I said, lowering my rice bowl. Japan? In the days since my enlistment, I hadn't given a thought to the unlikely possibility I'd be sent to Japan. Her son was leaving, disconnecting, and already my mother was scanning the outside world in hopes of understanding my future. I shook my head and said, "Not too many servicemen get sent Japan."

"Why you never write Japan on your paper?" she asked, her mouth beginning to hint at a smile.

"Paper?"

"The legal one you talk about. If get the chance, write Japan on that paper. Then you can go visit."

I smiled warmly, and she smiled back. We both looked toward my father. His mouth grew harder, tighter.

"One sugar worker," he spat, pushing away his bowl of rice. The ceramic bowl flipped upside down and vibrated on its rim, giving a circular voice to my father's disappointment. His voice spun round and round until my mother reached out and pressed the voice quiet. She tilted the bowl on its side and swept the spilled rice back into it with her napkin. Then she set the bowl in front of Dad, who lifted his chopsticks and resumed eating.

What kept my father's disappointment in perspective for me was the much greater disappointment of parents who would soon watch their graduating sons settle permanently into plantation life. At least I was getting away. During the days surrounding graduation, when my father ate less rice than usual, I knew that Marc Yamada's dad was barely eating at all.

Marc was a friend of mine who hadn't been accepted by the army because he weighed less than one hundred pounds. His weight seemed to me an odd reason to keep him out of the military. I knew grown men who were his size and smaller. Marc signed up, instead, for the sugar mill.

Meanwhile, the days to my departure began to pass. My dreams grew increasingly violent, startling me into full, conscious terror. I couldn't recall a similar period of such disturbing dreams, even in the restless months after Taizo died. As June turned to July I barely slept, slipping outside before sunrise to watch as sugar workers returned home after the night shift. Marc's work boots were already among those that trudged down our row toward home. Each morning I waved casually to him from the front steps. He nodded and continued walking. Somehow he knew the exact day I was leaving, and on that morning he stopped to talk.

"Promise one thing," he said, heading up my front walk.

"Anything," I answered, noting how easily his lunch can settled against his leg.

He lifted one knee and rested his boot on the step near my hip. "When you come back, tell me what I miss."

"Sure," I agreed, nodding.

"You going army for me, too," he said, reaching out with his hand to shake mine. His grip was surprisingly firm, like a workingman's. "After you come back," he continued, "we can try get the same shift."

I tried to keep a neutral expression, though inwardly I felt saddened by Marc's assumption that I'd one day join him at the mill.

"When you coming back?" he asked.

"Not sure," I said, stalling. "Not for long time."

"Anyway, can talk then."

"Till then," I agreed.

Marc walked away from my yard with an unusually straight back. His chin was forward and up, and his lunch can swung beside his leg with an already understood rhythm. We both knew he had missed his best chance to get away. By pretending that I'd come home and my life would continue on as before, he must have been trying to reconcile his own loss.

The sun had risen above Mount Haleakala and now appeared rooted to a thick layer of clouds. If one didn't know better, it would be possible to believe the clouds were holding onto the sun, holding back time, but within hours the sun was high in the sky, and I was waiting beneath the airport banyan tree for my flight to the island of Oahu. My mother and father held tickets for the same flight. They planned to witness my swearing-in that afternoon.

"You sure you can afford it?" I had asked my mother when she informed me they were coming.

"Can," she said, looking uneasily across the parlor toward Dad before adding, "We buy ticket with college money."

At the airport we conversed with Auntie Sachi and Uncle Toshi, who had come to see me leave. "Just no shame us old guys," Uncle instructed me. He held out rice crackers in a small bag so I could help myself to a handful. "Keep your uncle proud," he continued. "Us Hawaii servicemen was good at drinking beer."

Auntie elbowed him. "Drinking beer? That your only World War II fame, drinking beer?"

"Why not?" he said. "We won the war."

Auntie dismissed him with a wave of her hand. "Never mind him," she instructed me. "Just take care yourself."

"Never mind take care," Uncle retorted. "Drink beer. That way you can get plenty medal like me."

"Oh," said Auntie, "some plenty you brag."

He patted his stomach. "Somehow I no look like one serviceman already."

"Of course you no look like one serviceman," Auntie said. "Look your fat stomach."

"Beer and rice," said Uncle, rubbing his belly. "Both worth fat stomach."

A man at the gate interrupted with a boarding call. He then repeated his call, this time enhanced with a megaphone. I grabbed my satchel and tossed the strap over my shoulder. Mom adjusted her purse and picked up two rice bags, which I assumed hid the flower leis to be presented after my swearing-in ceremony. Dad carried the plane tickets.

Auntie hurried toward me and pulled an envelope from her purse. "Take care, Spencer," she said, pressing the envelope into my hand. I wondered how much money was inside. She hugged me, mentioning as we pulled apart that William was sorry he wasn't able to come.

"Never mind," I said, ignoring her lie. "You can tell him 'bye for me?"

She nodded and stepped aside to make way for her husband. Uncle Toshi shook my hand, pressing bills into my palm. The money was slipped so discreetly that I realized Auntie knew nothing about it. The official money was in the envelope, but Uncle was giving me extra.

"No shame the Fujii name," he said, more serious now. "Nobody can complain about us Hawaii men. Be proud your Japanese blood. Nothing for be shame about." He patted my shoulder forcefully, propelling me into a walk. Dad had already begun his stride toward the gate. Mom followed with the cumbersome rice bags and her purse.

I slipped between the two of them as we exited the terminal and walked into a heavy, moist wind. The wind was strong enough to be annoying, and when I turned my face from it, looking back over my shoulder, I noticed that Mom struggled with the windswept rice bags. She huddled against the wind, the rice bags lifting behind her. "I can carry them?" I asked, walking back to her. She agreed with an apologetic nod. Together we climbed the thin, metal stairs to the plane.

We had barely got the rice bags settled when the engines gathered strength and our small jet lifted away from the only land I'd ever touched. Soon I was above the central valley cane fields. Then I was higher than the peaks of Haleakala. Even as I watched out my window, amazed at this all-encompassing view of my island home, Maui disappeared. It was there beneath me, and then it was not, seemingly pulled underwater by the Pacific tides. I pushed back against my seat and craned my neck to confirm it was still there.

That afternoon on the lawn of the Hotel Street YMCA, I was sworn into the military with three hundred other enlistees from the Hawaiian islands. The date was an unforgettable July 4th, 1962. My parents stood in the audience along with the Hotel Street drunks and prostitutes who paused to watch.

After the ceremony, my mother followed my father through the crowd. Dad offered his hand in congratulations, and we shook. "Write your mother," he said. "No forget."

I nodded to him, then turned to Mom. She reached into one

of her rice bags and began the process of adorning me with leis. "This one from Mr. and Mrs. Sato," she said, straightening a carnation lei on my shoulders. "This one from Auntie Sachi and Uncle Toshi. She pick the best orchid from the garden." There were nearly twenty leis in all, each lei carefully explained and admired. The final lei, a maile, was from her and Dad. It was the only lei without explanation.

"Maile," I said, lifting the vine to my nose. "Where you got maile?"

She shrugged. "Mr. Medeiros brought back for me from Big Island." From her purse she pulled out a thick handful of white envelopes. "Long time before you get paid," she said. "Going need money."

I stuffed the envelopes into my satchel, quickly estimating that I had received hundreds of dollars. Our closest friends and relatives had given both leis and envelopes. Those not as close had given envelopes, but no leis.

"No forget keep track," my mother said. "Need for know how much money everybody give you. That way I can give same back."

"I can send you one list," I said.

"Make sure you no forget. Important. Some embarrassing if they give you and next time I forget for give them."

I nodded, well aware that Mom kept a written record going back to her wedding day of all gifts received by our family. Most gifts were cash, with the amounts determined by occasion and relationship. When the gifts weren't cash, they were edible. Giving too generous a gift was considered nearly as bad-mannered as giving no gift. Mrs. Okamoto was guilty of the former on at least one occasion, giving one hundred pounds of rice when twenty-five pounds would have been more appropriate.

"How I going pay back?" Mom asked Auntie Sachi after all the guests had left the party. "Why she give so much?"

"That one like for show off," Auntie said. "You see how she came late? Then she ask if plenty people can help carry present from her house. That way everybody can see her hundred-pound bag rice."

A military officer announced from the podium that it was time for the men to board the buses. My mother and I hugged, the leis a scented pillow between us. I got the urge to hug my father, but when I turned toward him with open arms, he stiffened. We had never hugged and would not begin now.

Mom's slightly cupped hand waved, then slowly lowered as I lined up with the others to board the buses for Schofield Barracks. She looked so tiny in the crowd, though many others were no larger. Her thin shoulders jerked with each inhale . . . exhale. She lifted her purse to her stomach and held it there with both hands.

It was to Dad I looked for the final good-bye. Carefully, he nodded. How can I explain the feeling, the rush of water behind my lids? To the non-Japanese it is difficult to explain a nod, the possible nuances in the tilt of a head. As I backed up toward the bus, keeping my place in line, I fastened my eyes on the hope in my father's face. I nodded to him, a bow to tradition, then turned on my heels, and boarded the bus. My neck pressed the leis against my seat as I remembered how tightly my mother had clutched her purse.

The bus ride to Schofield Barracks was short. "Get in formation! Get in formation!" the drill sergeant barked as we stepped from the bus. "Get those goddamned leis off your heads. What are you, a bunch of sissies? You're in the army now. Get those goddamned flowers outta your hair. You're nothin' but pineapples. Get in formation you bunch of goddamned Buddhaheads."

I threw my leis from my neck to the dirt. Hundreds of others also threw their leis, tearing them in haste. We trampled the leis as we scrambled into formation. The ground at our feet became a disturbing field of flowers.

Early the next morning we boarded our troop carrier at Pearl Harbor, Oahu. The eastern sky hinted toward sunrise, and I thought of how the sun would be lifting over Haleakala in a short while, coloring the clouds and gradually exposing the angles of Maui. I hadn't yet left Hawaii, but the island of Maui was already one hundred miles and millions of ocean waves away.

Even so, as the ship pulled away that morning, disturbing the flatness of the water, my separation from Hawaii felt strangely mutual. We were backing away from each other. I watched from the deck as the island of Oahu receded, then disappeared into a horizon of salty water. Would I ever return to Hawaii, to my family, to the pain of Taizo's grave? The rising conflict in Southeast Asia could kill me, and I was enormously fearful that the army could shame me. Because of Taizo, I knew shame and the desire to displace it. By comparison, death earned a spot on my mother's altar.

Our trip across the Pacific Ocean took five days and nights. Often I stood at the rear of the ship, looking back toward where we'd just been. On the third morning, when my eyes could barely stay open after a long night on fire duty, I tried to form in my mind a focused image of my parents. The clarity was unsatisfactory, as if blurred by layers of ocean waves. Each wave lifted and fell over their concerned faces in a wash of growing distance. I pushed away from the ship's rail and sighed.

"The carrots," ordered an officer behind me.

"Yes, sir," I said, hurrying to obey.

A rickety elevator took me down to the deep center of the ship, where I picked my way over sacks of rice and jugs of soy sauce. The eerie lack of motion in the ship's bowels troubled me, and I tried to ignore my fear that the ship was plummeting to the ocean floor. Was this what Taizo had felt before he drowned, this insistent fear of death? For the first time I wondered how long he held his breath before opening his mouth to the water. One minute, maybe? A ragged death preceded by exactly sixty seconds? Waves slapped against the ship, trapping me in their ferocious echoes. My blood pressure dropped in a whoosh of dizziness as I grabbed a sack of carrots and scrambled back to the elevator. I raised the lever that would activate the elevator, and a wild fear came over me that water could rush through the pores of the elevator shaft toward my own pores, water where there should be air. Silently, as the elevator ascended, I begged for land, any land, the land my brother couldn't reach.

Only when the elevator safely reached the deck did I realize I had been holding my breath. I hauled the bag of carrots to the kitchen and then wandered the deck in a slow, bewildered way, haunted by an image of Taizo opening his mouth to the water. Over and over I held my breath and counted to sixty, stopping only after I began to hear the remembered sound of water in my ears.

As I looked out across the deck to the Pacific, I thought it ironic that the ocean was the surface upon which I now traveled. As an island child, the ocean had been a life-long barrier. Though I had been warned about the tide beneath the surface, the power that could carry me somewhere far out to sea, what I saw were the ever-approaching waves that would bring me back to shore. I accepted ocean boundaries even as I questioned the cultural boundaries my parents tried to impose. Never did I seriously consider running away.

So I was taken by surprise when, shortly after arriving at Fort

Ord, the drill sergeant ordered us to get the idea of desertion "out of your slant-eyed heads. You got that?" he challenged a recruit who stood somewhere in the row behind me.

"I think so, sir," the recruit tentatively answered, summing up my own confusion.

"You think so? Who the hell ordered you to think? And you," he continued, turning to someone else. "Why in hell do these papers say you're Buddhist? You're no Jap."

A man with a deep, resonant voice said, "I get one Japanese great-grandma, sir."

That voice, I would later learn, belonged to Kenneth Kauai, a full-blooded native Hawaiian who had learned the Buddhist service was the only military-approved service located off base. On Sundays he stood in line and boarded the church bus with about seventy recruits of Japanese ancestry. Some of us hadn't been to a church service in years. Christian and Jewish men watched with envy as our bus drove away from base.

"You attending church?" Donald Toba asked me the first Sunday morning as our bus pulled away. We had met years earlier at a cousin's house in Lahaina. "Somehow I never thought you the type to go church," he persisted.

"I feeling religious," I said, annoyed we'd ever met.

Every Sunday morning he acted surprised to see me on the bus. Then, as boot camp neared completion, the army began authorizing passes to town that weren't contingent on attending Buddhist church. "What?" Donald said, searching me out in the barracks. "You not going church today?"

"Not today," I snapped, feeling guilty about having used my ethnicity to get off base.

He whirled toward Leonard Ichiriu. "What about you?" he accused. "You still going church?"

"Maybe next week," Leonard said.

"Church important," said Donald. He threw up his hands in disgust and hurried toward Roy Endo. The fact was, attendance at the Buddhist church dropped sharply.

You heard about the luau?" Kenneth asked, coming up from behind me one day near the end of training.

I continued to walk toward the barracks where I wanted to read a book. Kenneth again asked about the luau, and I nodded, aware that he and others were planning an elaborate Hawaiian feast for the last night of boot camp.

"Get kalua pig and everything," he said. "Poi, lau lau, rice, lomi lomi salmon. . . ."

"When they give the travel orders?" I asked, turning to face him.

Kenneth shuffled his boots and appeared confused. "Travel orders?"

"I like know for sure if I can go New Jersey."

Kenneth shrugged. "You heard we made one committee to cook the kalua pig? I looking for volunteers."

"Kenneth?" I asked, his name a clear question.

"What?"

"You feel like one American, the way the army says?"

"Why you asking me about that?" he said. "I thought we talking about kalua pig."

"I was wondering if you feel like one American."

His smile was calm. "Look my uniform, Spencer. Must mean something."

I shook my head slowly. "Sometimes I wore my grandpa's kimono, and that never mean nothing."

"Nothing?" asked Kenneth. "Must mean something. You one Japanese."

"Not exactly," I said, slipping away before Kenneth could say anything more about the luau. Right then, when the whole American continent was coming into view, I didn't want to focus on Hawaii.

The luau, without any help from me, began after sunset on our last night of boot camp. I was not feeling conversational and sat apart from the hundreds of men who had gathered. While it was true that my paper plate held foods of Hawaii, I could think of nothing but New Jersey. We had been given our travel orders and, as hoped for, I was leaving the next day for Fort Monmouth. Most specifically, I looked forward to standing in snow.

As a child, I had seen snow only from a distance. "You sure?" I asked my mother. "You sure not clouds?"

"Snow," she said, her face lifted toward the peaks of Haleakala.

"What it feels like?" I asked.

"I never touch."

"Marc Yamada get a bottle," I began. "He says inside the bottle get cloud, but I no see nothing. His dad went pig hunting up the mountain and caught cloud inside the jar."

"But no can see?" she asked curiously.

"Or touch," I said. "Marc only yell when I try take off the lid."

"Can still believe," said Mom, her eyes again on the snow in the distance.

I was visualizing that faraway snow, my luau plate forgotten on my lap, when, from across the lawn, a single voice began to rise above the collective chatter of the crowd. The first verse of "Aloha ʻOe" sailed toward me; the distinctive voice was Kenneth's. Others cleared an area around him as he sang the Hawaiian words written nearly a century earlier by Queen Lili ʻuokalani.

Then, with a dramatic pivot, Kenneth sang with his voice lifted toward the west. I realized he faced Hawaii. My forehead tightened with the understanding that at this time tomorrow I'd be even farther from home.

I set my plate on the grass, stood with my face toward home, and added my tentative voice to Kenneth's. Without turning, he lifted an arm toward me in acknowledgment. And then hundreds sang, and all eyes looked toward Hawaii, many of us whooping and shouting after the English words in the lyrics, ". . . until we meet again."

That night I fell asleep with alternating images of sugar cane and snow until they blended into one image of snow falling on cane. Only when I looked more closely at the image did I realize the snow was not snow, but falling grains of sugar. They glittered as they fell, landed on the cane, and stuck.

I must have brought the idea of snow into my dreams and out again, because in the moments just before awakening, I heard the long-forgotten voice of my second-grade teacher. She was trying to define the characteristics of winter to thirty confused children. "The clues are in the illustrations," she was saying. "For example, the falling snow means you must check the box marked *winter*."

I found the illustration of snow on my practice test and tried to connect it with the idea of winter. Beside me, Ed Kimura raised his hand and said, "Get one picture here with big rain. Not winter?"

"Absolutely not," the teacher said. "Remember, this will be a standardized test. Rain means *spring*."

This was getting confusing. I rubbed my forehead and determined to concentrate.

"Can each of you find the illustration with a pile of leaves?" she prompted. "If you look carefully, you'll notice the puffy-cheeked squirrel in the corner of the illustration. He is, of course, preparing for winter, a clue which means that this illustration represents *autumn*. That leaves us with the illustration of a sunny day, and we all know that the sun represents *summer*."

With my teacher's instructions thus recalled, I felt confident that I could identify autumn and winter, the two seasons most foreign to me. Yet, when I arrived in New Jersey that afternoon to begin my communications training, the colors of autumn brought me to a mesmerized standstill. I had never suspected colors like this. What came to mind was miles and miles of crayons left to melt beneath a Maui sun.

I felt awed by the leaves, but also cheated for having been wrong about autumn. That caused me to wonder what else I didn't know.

"Are you one of them Mexicans?" a strong, blond farmer type asked me that first night in our New Jersey barracks. I'd heard him referred to as Ole, a name unfamiliar to me.

"Japanese," I answered, aware that several other men had stopped to listen.

"Why are you in the United States military?" he asked, his eyebrows lifting into suspicious arches.

His were the first blond eyebrows I'd ever seen. I tried not to stare.

"I come from Hawaii," I clarified.

"You're Hawaiian, then," he announced to the semicircle that had now formed behind me.

I shifted my weight from one foot to the other. Hawaiian? In Hawaii we reserve the title "Hawaiian" for those of native Hawaiian ancestry. I had just explained to him I was of Japanese ancestry.

"Hawaii-born," I said, trying for the answer that would keep me honest.

"Tell me," said Ole, light-heartedly punching my shoulder, "are those hula girls as good as they look?"

In the hooting that followed I escaped the question. A Southern black named Sam described a kaleidoscope he once owned that featured a hula dancer on the inside cover. He could make her hips wiggle by turning the cylinder. That reminded Wally, a kid from either Iowa or Ohio—I could never keep those two straight—of a hologram that starred a hula dancer with a grass skirt. When he turned his wrist, the girl's grass skirt disappeared. He claimed he got it in a cereal box.

"You live in grass shacks?" Wally asked with an eager, innocent grin.

"A regular plantation house," I said, backing up so I was part of the semicircle.

"Grass shacks," said Wally.

"Hula dancers," Ole added. He rubbed his hands together and began his own attempt at hula, a gyrating motion that I could connect with no hula I'd ever seen. Ole sashayed up and down the center aisle, bumping his hips against the beds. Suddenly, I'd had enough.

"That all the better you can do hula?" I chided. "No hula dancer going stay around you."

His face turned as red as a drunkard.

"How'm I doing?" asked Wally, swishing his hips.

"I *know* a hula girl wants me," Sam claimed, making an attempt of his own as he sang about little grass shacks in Hawaii.

"Now you," said Ole, his arms crossed in an authoritative way.

"Me?" I asked.

He nodded aggressively. "Show me how you Hawaiians do it."

I saw no choice but to oblige, following the only two rules of hula I knew: bend the knees and roll the hips. Before long the others joined me in the aisle, swinging their hips. They all seemed to know the song about little grass shacks in Hawaii.

I wished I could escape, and the desire connected in memory to the day Mr. Okamoto caught me stealing mangoes. Then, too, I had wanted to escape, and it was Taizo who had found the courage to lead me away. I had thought my brother brave, but what had he known of worlds without sugar cane, without rice? He had measured me so eagerly against our fields of cane, never once considering the validity of the measuring stick.

What, I wondered, had Ole measured himself against? A field of wheat? The side of a red-painted barn?

"Ole," I said, interrupting the swish of his hips. "When I was small, the sugar cane grew all around. My older brother and me would try see which was more tall—the sugar cane or us. You ever did that? You ever measured yourself against something?"

"The corn," he said, squinting. "It grew taller than me at a different time every year, all depending on the rain. You ought to come and see the corn in August."

Someone who had been listening from a top bunk leaned his skinny face over the edge and spoke rapidly. "We had a wall in the kitchen," he said, peering down at us. "Every year on my birthday, Dad measured me and added a new mark on the wall. He had a special name for it, called it my 'high-water mark.'" The face then disappeared from above us as quickly as it had appeared.

"I had a big brother," Wally said, "which works as good as a kitchen wall." He smiled, displaying his crooked teeth. "Made him stand back to back with me till I nearly drove him crazy. Passed him up, too, when I was sixteen, which was hard for him to take." He scratched his head and added, "Couldn't get him to measure against me after that."

"A tree," said Sam wistfully. He tilted his face toward the ceiling and sighed. "A magnolia tree in our front yard."

I was flown to Saigon the following spring. It was 1963, a time when Vietnam was still far from most American minds. Years would pass before the United States would be connected to Vietnam by daily news body counts and the Kent State killings. The years I spent as a photographer in Vietnam were the years that quietly stirred those that followed. The famous images of the war, such as the gun at the Vietnamese man's head, the naked girl running from napalm, those were the honest records. Mine were generally photographs taken with fake light.

Ready?" I asked, looking down into the viewfinder of my camera. In the year since arriving in Saigon, I had asked that same question of hundreds of men.

The general assumed a stiff, stern pose. "All set," he said.

I pressed the shutter, confident of an adequate result.

"Two more," said the general. "Make me look good."

I pulled out the negative cartridge and slid another into the camera. Four-by-five negatives ensured quality in the enlarged prints, as clear as a general's order.

"How's this?" the general asked, pulling back his shoulders.

"Right there, sir," I said. "Your chin a little more to the left. . . ."

Nearby, a government dignitary from the State Department straightened his collar in the reflection of a framed print. MACV headquarters had been busy all morning. Here, away from the Vietnamese jungles, men could arrange their collars, their buttons, the lifts of their well-shaven chins. I had recently spent a few weeks dangerously north while another photographer had taken his leave, and I was grateful to be back at MACV, where dignified men could arrange themselves.

Few are natural in front of the lens, and the point was crystallized for me when I photographed a dying soldier during my weeks up north. Blood trickled from the man's nose and mouth. Even so, I might have continued without pause if I hadn't noticed the blood running from his ear. I stood over him, wanting to collapse, wishing I could scream, when he blinked to prove life.

"No worry. You going be okay," I said. "We sent for help."

His lips flexed in a moaning grimace.

"You mind if I take your picture?" I asked, as if I were scheduling an appointment. Methodically I knelt, steadied my hands, and bent forward to narrow the distance between us. His twisted limbs made a startling composition within the frame. The trunk of his body lay in a neat diagonal. It wasn't until later, when I developed the photo in our makeshift darkroom, that I saw the smile on the dying man's face, a smile for the photographic record.

Though I didn't like to think about that smile after I returned to Saigon, I made the mistake of describing the experience to Winston Medeiros, a Hawaii serviceman who typed reports at MACV. Winston began to press me for details.

"You only think you like know," I warned him. The two of us were wandering up and down the streets of Saigon, where the modest buildings reminded me of Wailuku town. What didn't remind me of Wailuku were the ever-present Vietnamese prostitutes, dressed in white, who signaled to us with their fingers and eyes. We ignored a girl's throaty invitation as she neared and passed us. Along the row of shops to our right, owners had set up outdoor tables. Several of them called out to Winston and me. One owner hurried around his table and grabbed my arm, hopeful I'd consider his wares as he fast-talked in Vietnamese. His language and its force reminded me of the childhood scoldings I had withstood in Chinese Camp: the clashing consonants, the jammed vowels, the words spit from the throat. I pulled my arm free so that Winston and I could continue.

"Crazy," said Winston.

"Desperate," I agreed, while, behind us, the vendor continued to scold with sentences that exploded arbitrarily. The debris of words fell in a shower on my back. I shrugged and visualized the words falling from my uniform to the ground for others to step on.

"One thing I keep wondering," said Winston, whose ancestry was a combination of Portuguese and Filipino. "If somebody find us dead, without our dog tags and uniforms, would they identify us as American?"

"Without my uniform?" I said. "What I going be doing without my uniform?"

"Say the uniform gets blown off," he said, speaking as casually as is possible when mentioning bombs.

I rolled my eyes. "Only if the American that find us comes from Hawaii, he going know," I said. "At least you taller than me. For sure they going think I one Vietnamese."

"Then you better hope I find you," said Winston, with what started to be a grin. While I watched, though, it changed to a knowing, tight sigh.

"My grandpa live with us when I was one small boy," I told Winston. "Plenty time I try on his best kimono. Had the sash and everything. One time he even let me hold his samurai sword. The kimono never did feel right, even when I grew up and try it again. Then, when I came in the military, my uniform was way too big. Even though we had one all-Hawaii company, the army order same size uniform they always order. They give me one large size uniform. I had to tuck the pants inside my boots."

Winston took a big step backward in order to study my uniform. "Fits now," he noted.

"They finally give me one medium," I said. "Fits better than any kimono ever did."

"Maybe they can recognize you," said Winston, twisting his lips.

"Huh?"

"If they find you dead, I mean. Someone would shout, 'Get one American over here.'"

"You think so?" I asked, but when pressed that far, Winston fell silent. I opened my mouth to ask again, but he shook his head to stop me. One side of his mouth tightened in a sorrowful way, as if he couldn't bring himself to answer.

PHOTOGRAPHS

The army asked me where I wanted to go upon discharge. It was the first question of any consequence the army had asked during my years of military service, and I found that decisions were easier when I could blame others for the possible results. The lieutenant held a clipboard and asked me where I planned to go in the factual way that a person might ask for my rank or the color of my eyes. When I didn't immediately answer, he tapped his clipboard with the point of his pen and looked toward the ceiling.

I had been temporarily lost in thought the way a Wainoa boy gets temporarily disoriented in a field of cane. "Home, sir," I said and, having answered, again pulled away in thought. I was aware of slipping behind glazed eyes.

He lowered his clipboard and blew air through his clenched teeth, snapping my eyes into focus. "I'm not a mindreader, Fujii," he barked.

"Maui, sir," I clarified, and watched as the lieutenant scribbled my destination. In a muscular sigh, my face tightened, relaxed. The decision was made. More daring servicemen were choosing California, citing low-cut bathing suits and veteran-friendly community colleges, but I had decided that I wanted the simpleness of home. I had not been back in three years and missed the familiar.

The night before I left Saigon I sat on my bed sorting hundreds of eight-by-ten photos. I had taken too many similar photos of women washing their dishes and clothes at water holes, while their naked children splashed nearby. My photos were of civilians, except for a few group shots taken in New Jersey and Saigon. I already regretted not having a camera when I was in basic training, though I did receive one long, official photo of our all-Hawaii company. I picked it up from the bed and was disconcerted to realize it was the same shape as the funeral pictures in my mother's altar. Had any of these men died in service to their country? The invisible presence of a coffin began to materialize in the center of the photo. I rolled the photo closed, fastened it with a rubber band, and tossed it aside.

From the glossies on the bed I sorted the group shots to keep, including an informal pose of five guys in bright white T-shirts. Three sat on a bed and two leaned against the adjacent end table. Their smiles toward the camera were genuine. Only Wally was left-handed; everyone else held his cigarette with his right. Ole, the fellow with the widest smile, lifted an empty wine glass.

I blinked away the faces of my friends as I added the photo to a pile in a small box. Next I selected from the bed a formal group shot taken at the completion of photography school, a photo I propped against my pillow to study. A professional had shot the group of us in formal dress greens. We stood like soldiers who have been ordered to be "at ease." On the clapboard building behind us a sign read, "Combat Surveillance Photographs." I was the only Japanese American.

I slid the photo into the box and thumbed through a whole stack of photos that meant nothing special to me, tossing them carelessly to the floor.

My memory shifted as I came across a photo of Korean children in the countryside. I had nearly completed my two-week leave and was tired of taking photographs, but the boys spotted my camera. I couldn't deny them. The six little boys, at the age of missing front teeth, grinned. The photo captured their laughter as they saluted the military man with the camera.

I threw it into the box and flung several others to the floor. My eyes scanned across glossies of sculpted rice paddies and open-air markets. I chose some, discarded others, and worked my way down to the last photo upon my bed. I would keep the picture of three young women who looked at the camera but did not smile.

The woman in the center of the photo wore silk, while the other two wore blouses and skirts in the casual American style, complete with chain belts at the waist. Their short hair was neatly trimmed. The one on the right gave my friend a venereal disease and appeared to have known more pain than the other two, whose faces were soft.

I had spent two evenings with the woman on the left. "More beer?" she asked in the smoky, dark Korean bar where we first had met. This was the last night of my leave, and I knew I'd go home with her again.

"No more beer," I said, indicating with a motion toward the door that I was ready to go.

The walk to her thatched-roof house was short, but outside the sleet fell toward us in diagonal lines. She leaned against my side, and I hunched my shoulders to protect us both.

The floor of her clay home was warm, heated by a fire that burned in the crawl space beneath it. We removed our clothes and stood face to face. Our bodies met before we sank in a joint kneel to the floor. In the chill of recovery we lay with impersonal distance between us, warmed only by the floor.

I laid that picture on top of the others I wished to keep. A thought came to mind that at some later date I would again sort through the photos, further honing the memories. Some photographers need a logical reason to discard a photo. For me, a gut reaction is enough.

I slept restlessly during that last night in Vietnam, under-standing the tossing and turning had something to do with the photographs, but not precisely what. Perhaps my tension related to the careless discarding of photos that had seemed worth recording at the moment of the camera's snap.

Our plane headed across the Pacific, and this time I was going home. As a child, I had never imagined the round trip, never considered that a Pacific crossing could mean a return to Maui. The plane stopped for refueling in Honolulu, where about a dozen of us got off. The rest were continuing on to the main-land. I watched from my seat as a cross-section of Hawaii's men headed up the aisle, and I guessed many of their childhoods by the colors of their skin, the shapes of their eyes, the frames of their bodies. There on the plane, I easily could have divided them into the rows that some would return to.

I was the last of the Hawaii men to step into the aisle. My eyes swept up and down the plane at faces of those who had become my friends and now were going back to the mainland. I picked out my closest friends and shook hands. Those parting handshakes were the tight grips of muscled fingers and under-stood endings. My toned body tightened like muscles around my ragged emotions so that when I loudly called "aloha," backing with large strides up the aisle of the plane, my voice held steady.

I had just turned my back when some of the men called "aloha" to me from their seats. I recognized the accents and pitches of individual voices. Because I did not turn around, the word fell upon my back, my heels, the flesh at the nape of my neck.

"Aloha," I said quietly, repeating the word in a whisper. I was almost home, with only a few more good-byes to endure. Leave-takings had unsettled me ever since my brother's death, the way they nearly always left edges hanging. I yearned for the good-bye as crisp as an honor guard's salute.

From the airport we caught a bus to Schofield to receive our official discharge papers. Part of the process included turning in clothing and supplies to the quartermaster. I was the last of our group to get in line, and I was beginning to wonder why others were in more of a hurry to get home than I was. The long line of men turned to scan the new additions to it. I saw a few faces I recognized from basic training.

"Hey, how you?" one man said.

Another called from his place in line, "You mean those short legs of yours made it back? Better tell the drill sergeant."

"My legs not short," I said. "The pants was too long."

"We all made it back," called a third man near the front of the line, stretching out his arm in a handshake position. He obviously didn't want to jeopardize his position in line by walking back to shake my hand. A quick look over my own shoulder confirmed that as the last person in line, I had no position to guard.

I walked all the way forward and began to handshake my way

down the line. Each man without exception reached out to shake my hand. When I had nearly returned to my unenviable position in line, the door pushed open and a returning soldier stepped into the room. Kenneth Kauai paused just inside the doorway and scanned the line of men. His eyes clicked into place as he recognized me.

"Spencer!" he called, striding over with his arm out-stretched. Kenneth had lost weight during the past few years, further emphasizing the broad shoulders and strong facial bones of his Hawaiian ancestry. I thought him handsome in a classic way. My hand reached out toward his while my feet secured what would no longer be the last place in line. We shook hands warmly as he lined up behind me. "You going Maui?" he asked.

"Today," I said, taking a step forward as the line moved. "How about you?"

"Catching the next flight for Hilo." His face leaned forward over my shoulder and he said in a low voice, "By the way, we need for turn in our raincoat?"

I nodded, turning to face him. "Have to."

"What if no get?" he asked.

"Gotta pay," I said, looking forward again. I stretched back my neck toward him and added, my chin toward my chest, "What, you lost your raincoat?"

"Threw it away," he said, chuckling. "I never thought I need turn it in."

"Hard luck," I agreed.

We moved forward slowly, and others joined at the back of the line. I had nearly reached the table where I'd turn in all but my underwear, the fatigues I was wearing, and my dress greens, in case of recall, when Kenneth's face leaned forward over my shoulder again and he half-whispered, "You can give me your raincoat."

"I only get one," I quietly protested. Generosity is a virtue highly regarded in Hawaiian society, and I felt Kenneth was unfairly using that against me. Still, I figured I'd keep the raincoat.

"*After* you turn yours in," he whispered. "Look the pile behind the table. When you walk around that side, grab it and pass it to me."

"What if get caught?" I said, turning to show him the uneasy look in my eyes.

"Easy for take," he said. "Nobody will notice."

I stepped up to the table and returned my items. The quartermaster made checks on an elaborate chart that was Scotch-taped to the table between us. His assistant tossed the items into individual piles on the floor behind the table. I was given the go-ahead, and Kenneth stepped up for his turn. He glanced over and smiled at me as I rounded the table, presumably so I wouldn't feel guilty about the raincoat.

By then, though, it was too late, because I had already decided to retrieve it for him. I lifted the top raincoat from the pile and passed it to Kenneth beneath the corner of the table.

He casually slipped it to the quartermaster, who made a check-mark in the raincoat category.

Outside Kenneth said, "You not bad for one Buddhahead."

"No talk," I said. "You one Buddhahead, too."

Kenneth laughed gorgeously, a massive laugh that matched the size of his shoulders. "We home, Spencer."

I nodded. "Now you can have kalua pig for dinner."

"How you knew?" he said. "My family is making me one luau tonight."

"Plenty beer then," I said, grinning.

"Yeah, plenty. And what? Your family not making you one party?"

"Maybe," I said, although I knew it was unlikely. I had wanted to see their honest emotions when I returned, rather than the planned, and had not written them of my discharge.

"Hey, I went school with that guy," said Kenneth, pointing across the room. "Call me when you come Hilo-side. We can go Buddhist church together."

The laughter was loose, the handshake tight. As he strode toward his friend, I knew it was unlikely I'd ever call him. I took one last look at Kenneth, then hurried to the paymaster for my final military paycheck.

A few hours later I was aboard a small, interisland plane bound for Maui. I watched from my window for my home island to appear, the tall green mountains, the gradual edges of shoreline, the cliffs, the cane, the waterfalls, the black lava rock, the land the Hawaiians call ʿāina. My nose pushed against the glass as I studied the spaces among clouds for the horizon of Maui's land.

When the island first edged into focus, one huge field of green, I pressed both hands against the window on either side of my face to get as close as possible. Waves glided toward her shores, sparkling like the newly fallen snow of New Jersey that I had been able to touch on my journey away from home.

Our plane neared the island, and from above I was reminded that its shape, similar to the head and shoulders of a sculpted bust, had inspired the nickname "Mother Maui." The image soothed me, that soon I could lay my head in the lap of the island.

We continued our descent over fields of sugar cane that I realized I had never seen. In the years that I had been gone, each field had completed an entire cycle and begun again. I knew my father was somewhere below, perhaps hidden among the rows of tall cane. He would be wearing a large hat to shield his face from the sun. If he was down there, now, looking up, he had no way of knowing I was aboard this plane. My stomach clutched with the sudden thought that it would have been kinder to have written my parents about my return.

I was, of course, not greeted at the airport. I could have phoned any number of people who by now owned cars, including Uncle Toshi, but that would have ruined the surprise and, besides, I no longer thought a dozen miles a difficult walk.

I threw my duffel bag over my shoulder and took my first steps toward home.

I hadn't got far when someone recognized me. The car screeched to a stop about ten yards down the road, then backed up until parallel with me. "Spencer?" the gruff voice called out through the open passenger window. "That you?"

The car was not familiar, but I knew the voice. Mr. Okamoto was not among those I had wished to see. I walked up to the passenger side of the car and leaned my elbows on the window ledge. "I just came back from the service," I said stupidly, for Mr. Okamoto kept careful track of everyone's business and would surely know where I had been.

"Get in," he ordered.

"I can walk. Not far."

"Get in," he repeated with the authority of his age.

Cursing beneath my breath, I threw my belongings in the back and sat in front. "Thanks for stopping," I said.

"Nice for see you," he mumbled. He questioned me as he drove, pretending it was nothing but idle conversation. With Mr. Okamoto, words always carried intent. "Your parents know you coming back?" he asked.

"No," I said, shifting in my seat.

"No wonder I never hear," he said.

This was not how I had envisioned my return home. "Can pull over?" I said.

"Nonsense. Not home yet."

I slapped my hand on the dashboard. "Pull over. I can walk home."

He slammed on the brakes, throwing my chest into the dashboard. "Even the army no can teach you respect," he said. "You still the shame of your parents. After your brother die, you suppose to be the oldest boy. But look at you. No respect for anybody."

I grabbed my things from the back seat and slammed the car door shut behind me. Then I whirled around and said through the open window, "Let me take your picture."

"My picture?"

I spoke deliberately. "I know you. I can take your picture better than anybody. Get out of the car and come over here."

Curiously, he obliged. "Go where?" he said, coming around the front bumper.

"There," I said, pulling the camera from my duffel bag. "No need do anything. Just look at the camera."

I knelt so that he'd be forced to look down, a physical manifestation of the man's character. He appeared unnaturally large from my position, the way he appeared when I was a little boy with mangoes in my shirt. His chin shaded the sunlight from his neck and emphasized the grim jut of his jaw.

"You finish?" he demanded. "Get things for do."

I pulled out the top of my shirt and blew some cool air down my chest. "Done," I said, sitting down in the grass at the side of the road.

"Then better be going," he snapped. "You coming?"

"No, you go on."

He nodded, grumbled something I couldn't hear, and headed for the driver's side.

"Mr. Okamoto?" I asked.

"What now?" he complained.

"Something happen to your leg? You look like you have some kind of limp."

"Fell from the damn mango tree," he said, "trying for collect the fruit."

"Not getting too old for climbing trees?" I asked.

"You not so young yourself," he grumbled before he got in his car and drove away.

I watched until he was out of sight, pushed myself up from the ground, and walked toward home with the wind nudging at my face. I still had several miles to go.

When I reached the first roadside cane field, I stopped to touch the stalks. Then I knelt and rubbed the pads of my fingers in the soil, pressing my hands flat upon the dirt. With my knees and hands in the soil, I looked up to watch the fluid way that cane moves in the wind.

I crossed to where the ocean laps the Maui shore. Gradually, the tips of my fingers easing in, I reached into the Pacific, catching her water with the palms of my cupped hands. My hands relaxed, and the water seeped through my fingers. I scooped more water and lifted my cupped hands above me in the air, tilting them toward my face and neck. The water trickled down into the pattern of my fatigues.

Then I started up the Wainoa cane road that would lead me home. The road was longer than I remembered, each step upon it more thoughtful. The cane, careful in its pauses, dipping at the waist, waved me home.

My eyes shifted from side to side at the fields that lined either side of the road. The field to my right was taller than that to my left. I reached my arms straight out, then lifted the right arm to the level of that field, the left a bit lower, so that I resembled a child playing airplane. My step became lighter. I twirled a circle in my army boots and began to run. I ran past the mill, which blew smoke over the camps. The glare of the strong sun made it appear as if the various conveyers were undulating down the sides of the mill. I blinked away both the glare and undulation. As I rounded the mill, the air smelled thickly sweet. I took it purposely into my lungs and held it all the way to the road that led to Japanese Camp. There, I let out the air in one long sigh, and started the last stretch home.

Ladies began to wave from their yards and porches. They called my name. "Spencer," one lady called, and "Fujii-san," called another. I nodded politely, but was careful not to take the slightest step toward either of them. The close boundaries of plantation life had motivated a series of complicated manners, one of which was that you did not speak to someone who did not want conversation. Had I taken even a step toward one of the ladies, she in turn could have walked toward me and begun talking.

I considered myself home when I first smelled the flowers spread across and beneath our plumeria tree. Their tropical scent passed through the filter of Wainoa and came to me, came for me. I noted where individual plumerias lay, where the wind and their falls had carried them. One flower balanced on a single, folded petal.

The tree was a common plumeria, and it was the common that I had returned to see. I knelt and lifted one of the white and yellow flowers to my nose. Where, I wondered, looking up the front steps, was Mom?

I would have first thought to check the house, but I heard a scratchy noise and found her raking leaves in the backyard. She appeared momentarily unsettled, confused, then carefully set down the rake and walked over to take my hand. "When you came back?" she asked, holding my hand tightly, looking up my shoulder to my eyes.

"Only now."

"I never knew you was coming. Why you never told?"

"I thought a surprise was better," I said.

She nodded, then took a few steps back and openly studied me. "Some big you came," she said, shaking her head as if I were a puzzle she couldn't understand.

"I was skinny before," I gently reminded her. "Besides, in the army can eat all I want. They no care how much I like eat."

She giggled. "Guess I better cook plenty for dinner. Better go market quick."

"Not yet," I said, pulling open my duffel bag and reaching in for my camera. "Stay right there and no move."

"Where else you think I going?" she said. "Not in the army like you, going all around the world."

"No," I said, trying with a flex of my hand to hold her in place, "No move at all."

Puzzled, she shook her head, and I got the idea that with each shake of her head she hoped her thoughts would sift into place. She watched cautiously as I looked down into my Mamiya camera.

"Look this way," I said. The angle was good and I almost took the shot, but the sun fell unfairly harsh on her curious face. I took a few steps to the left, looked up from the camera, and asked, "You can sit instead on the steps?"

She puckered her lips. "I thought I not suppose to move."

"Never mind that," I said, laughing. "I change my mind."

"You lucky you just came back," she said, limply pointing her finger. "Otherwise, I not going have time for this." She walked over to the stairs and sat upon the middle step. "How this?" she asked.

"Perfect. I just need few props."

"Props?" she said, her face wrinkling in confusion. "What kind props you need?"

"Stay right there. No move."

"I not going anywhere," she reminded me for the second time that afternoon.

I ran to the front porch and grabbed all the shoes and slippers neatly lined up before returning to the backyard.

"What the shoes and slippers for?" Mom asked.

"My props, these," I explained, lining them up in what I thought was an artistic way on the stairs.

"What you putting shoes all around me for?"

"Never mind. You can take off your slippers?"

"Take off my slippers? No, I not going take off. Shame, that. I stay outside. Why take off my slippers?"

"I want you in bare feet."

"Bare feet?" she said, looking down at her toes. "What if not clean?"

"Your feet always clean," I said.

Even as she shook her head, she took off her slippers. I set them at the foot of the stairs.

"Crazy, this," she said, hands on her hips. "No show anybody else this picture."

"Front page of *Life Magazine*," I said, grinning.

She looked up then, about to protest, her mouth slightly open, her head at a thoughtful tilt, and I caught it for all time. At the moment when the shutter clicked, one of my mother's bare feet pressed flat on the bottom step and the other flexed toward the camera. The flexed foot demonstrated an unnaturally large space between the big toe and the next toe, a space nudged open by the thongs of many slippers. The bottom of the foot was clean.

My mother was the only family member I was able to surprise by my return. Mr. Okamoto predictably notified my father and uncle with a special trip to the mill, and, of course, I had seen many people on my walk through the camps. The return of a local boy from overseas was something to talk about.

My father returned from work that afternoon no more quickly than usual, pulling his boots off on the front steps, then continued on toward where I waited in the doorway. I held open the screen door as he stepped inside.

"Spencer," he said, nodding once as I pulled shut the door behind him.

"Dad."

"You came back."

"For little while."

"Where you going next?"

"Not sure," I said. "I could go Honolulu."

He nodded thoughtfully, then straightened. "No stay here too long," he said.

I nodded, already aware that I had no choice but to leave. If I had decided to stay in Wainoa and work in the cane fields, my father's disappointment would have sent me to the dormitory housing for single men who couldn't get along with their parents.

That evening I took Dad's photograph as he ate from his rice bowl. I was able to proceed slowly, shifting angles, studying the light, because he easily ignored the camera. One hand held his rice bowl beneath his chin, while the other hand guided chopsticks into the bowl, lifting the rice to his mouth. Each time he lifted the chopsticks from the bowl, the rice balanced in a tiny pyramid on the way to his mouth. When I took the photo, I spotted a grain of rice on the edge of my father's lip that I thought might flaw his dignity. Later I considered retouching the photo, but in the end I left the dangling grain of rice upon his lip. I was still childish enough to hope that someday my father would see the photo and the rice would bother him.

In the week that followed I took other photos, limiting each subject to exactly one press of the shutter. I had grown weary of generals who didn't understand that the first photo was usually my best. Auntie was hanging clothes when I approached with the camera. I think she had been looking forward to her turn. She lay a wet pillow case across the top of her head and rested her folded arms upon that. The strange photo brings to mind a Japanese woman in sheikh headgear, beneath a clothesline of laundry. Her teeth glitter.

The next photo I took was of Uncle. He held a bottle of beer, which he raised to his forehead in a salute. The photo catches a word between his lips, and leaves one to wonder over the word. He looks to be a happy man. His shoulders and smile are pleasantly balanced.

William was the most difficult to lure before the camera. I

felt it an unfair intrusion to catch him unaware and asked him to choose the time and place. He was in high school, now, with a voice lower than I remembered.

"The reservoir," he said when he was ready for me to take his photograph.

"The reservoir?" I asked, stunned.

"You said you want one honest picture."

"The reservoir, then," I agreed, my stomach clutching.

William began walking. "I never went back since that day," he said.

"Me neither," I said, following his purposeful gait through cane fields to the deep reservoir, a mountain stream that the plantation dammed for cane irrigation. Peering into the water I said, "Looks so calm now. No wonder it never look scary to young boys."

"I was scared," said William. "No forget that."

I faced him, the water now behind my back. "But I caught you," I reminded him. "No forget I caught you."

"I never forgot," said William. "No matter how I try, I never forgot."

"Some things not suppose to forget," I said.

"Why you think I wanted to take the picture here?" he asked in a voice that chilled me. "Now you can have one permanent record."

"Can wait till later," I said.

"Take it," said William, facing me directly.

I looked down into the camera, then tilted it back because William was now taller than I. Through the lens I watched him stare forcefully into my face while he said, "I did what you said. I never told the truth."

I snapped the shutter when his face was at once earnest and angry. The look in his eyes stretched toward mine, and the stretch carried with it an immeasurable anger. I lowered the camera and said, "No one else was there. Only us know."

William said quietly, "You took my childhood."

"I took nothing," I said, and suddenly felt tired. So much of life was behind me, now. I felt the weight of the past upon my shoulders, pushing me down toward the ancient position of my ancestors. My body scrunched into a deep bow at the lip of the reservoir. There, I let flow the water of my eyes, conscious of the deadly water behind me, and conscious, also, of William lifting the camera from beside my foot. He took a photo of my pain, as I had taken his. I heard the camera click.

CAROLINE

I moved to Honolulu and got hired as a photographer for the daily newspaper. I suppose I should have thanked Mr. Okamoto for the position. During the job interview, when I displayed my photography portfolio for the managing editor, he particularly liked the photo of Mr. Okamoto alongside his Buick. He noted my ability to catch the candid, a talent essential for the position. I guess he thought the old man's grimace was temporary, and that somehow I had the genius to catch it.

I spent many hours in government buildings attending tedious meetings, my camera aimed at the heads of men behind lecterns. Other duties included staking out the areas near male bathrooms for the photos of department heads. Lower-level civil service employees posed eagerly at their desks. Their secretaries often tried to get in the background of the photos, angling shorthand pads away from their faces, pushing hair from their eyes. When they succeeded, we cropped them out.

Individual photos were kept for years by the editorial staff, showing up repeatedly in the pages of our newspaper. If the accompanying story was a paper-selling edition of corruption and fraud, I was sent to get a current photo. In too many of those situations, the official used his accumulated vacation time to hide from my camera, forcing the paper to run a photo of a youthful college graduate when the guy was by now bald and middle-aged. I always wondered how his wife felt about that.

I met Caroline when she joined the newspaper in the mid-seventies as a reporter. She had recently arrived from the mainland with a smile that girls in Japanese camp weren't allowed to have. I liked her fearless "hello" and the way she looked me directly in the eye. Yet she understood the idea of boundaries, of lines drawn firm, which I had found lacking in many of the Caucasian women I had met. She didn't push at either me or my emotions. I willingly gave both to her.

In the beginning of our relationship I wanted her more than she wanted me. I watched closely as her smile changed, an open stretch, a flex of joy, and we planned the years ahead. We married despite the objections of every person who loved either of us. The years since have been worth the disappointment we caused.

I do not know how or what other men think of their wives. I ponder only my own. Sometimes I feel that the sun's rays fall more kindly upon Caroline than upon others, casting her in an open, honest light. How else to explain the lack of shadows upon her face? My mother grew to love her, and I have been left to wonder if my father might have loved her, too. For Caroline, I would marry again. Her black hair shines. Her blue eyes glitter. When she walks in that carefree way of hers, the light goes with her.

Regarding that light: sometimes I purposely turn it off. The glare gets to me.

Of what do we argue? Rice and potatoes. They are the physical crux of our ancestries, the food of our souls. When we announced our plans to marry, our parents pleaded with us to find someone of our own race. No one even mentioned rice or potatoes.

Caroline's dad didn't want a "Jap" in the family, having fought against them in World War II. Her wartime descriptions of my Uncle Toshi, a member of the highly decorated 442nd Regimental Combat Team, meant nothing. She told of other Hawaii men who had broken Japanese codes, but that meant even less to him. He claimed he might have killed some of my ancestors, if lucky.

My mother's biggest fear was that when I eventually had children, Caroline would secretly take them to the U.S. mainland and never come back. I'd never touch my children again. I nearly said in frustration that a person doesn't have to take a child to the mainland to give them away. The words came to my lips, but not past. My mother's hunched shoulders stopped them.

Other reasons given to keep us from marrying included the skin color of our children, our ten-year age difference, and our differing religions, none of which has caused much concern in our fifteen-year marriage. The basic values of our totally different upbringings are strikingly similar. We are too consistent in most respects to be used against each other by our children.

We were married in the Honolulu courthouse on April 14, 1979. After all those years as a newspaper photographer, I felt comfortable in government buildings. The particular wedding date we had chosen meant nothing, other than that we were willing to wait no longer. I was already in my mid-thirties and tiring of a bachelor's Waikiki life.

On the impersonal sidewalk in front of the courthouse, while strangers stared, I draped Caroline's shoulders with a maile lei. She inclined her head and watched my eyes intimately as I lifted the length of her hair and positioned the maile.

Our families, still hoping our minds could be changed, did not know of our wedding until it had taken place. We stood before the judge, and two court workers halfheartedly witnessed our vows. The marriage didn't turn me away from my ancestry, as my father had feared, but, surprisingly, toward it. For the first time I understood that I was the only keeper of a long family history, that only I could pass it on. Caroline would have her own ancestral stories to tell.

The small issues in our marriage have proven to be the most difficult. It still bothers me how Caroline determines whether a baked potato is ready to be eaten; it was, in fact, the subject of our first disagreement. She reached into the oven with a fork and poked the potatoes to check if they were ready.

"What you doing?" I asked, watching over her shoulder.

She continued to mercilessly jab and prod the potatoes. "I'm checking to see if the potatoes are ready," she said in a voice that echoed from the oven.

"What you using a fork for?"

She straightened, pushed shut the oven door, and turned to face me. "That's how you know if they're ready."

"Not suppose to use a fork," I told her. "Suppose to use one chopstick."

"Chopstick?" she asked, her face wrinkling in disbelief. "Chopsticks are for sukiyaki or something. Why would anyone use a chopstick to test a baked potato?"

"Only makes one hole," I explained. "The fork makes too many holes."

Her eyes flashed incredulously. "*You* are going to tell *me* how to cook potatoes?"

"Only if you do it wrong," I told her.

I'm glad she didn't have a potato in her hand. She might have thrown it at me.

Conversely, several years passed before Caroline accepted that I was the family expert on rice and wanted to eat rice with all my dinners, no matter the menu.

"But we're having spaghetti," she protested early in our marriage. "Who needs rice with spaghetti and garlic bread?"

"Me," I said, washing the rice.

"That will be three starches," she reasoned. "Nobody needs three starches at one sitting."

"Without rice," I said, "the meal is only a snack. I want dinner."

As we ate dinner that evening she asked, "Why'd you cook so much rice?"

"In case you like some," I said.

We flew to Maui for introductions shortly after our marriage. As we stepped into the small parlor of my parents' house, I took Caroline's hand in mine. "Mom, Dad, this is Caroline."

My wife smiled nervously. "I've been waiting to meet you," she said.

"Us, too," said my mother, forcing a smile. "Nice for meet you."

Dad nodded abruptly and left the room.

With him gone I relaxed slightly, though Caroline's back pushed against the screen door, bowing it. I guessed by the way my mother's eyebrows rose that she was waiting for me to speak.

"You get room for us to stay?" I asked her. "If not, we can go hotel."

"A hotel would be no trouble at all," added Caroline. "We'd still have a lot of time to get acquainted."

Mom's eyes clouded in confusion. She glanced down the hallway to the kitchen, where Dad could be heard opening and closing cupboards, then turned back toward us. "We get plenty room," she said, feigning enthusiasm. "Get your suitcase and bring inside."

We carried to the house our suitcase and the cooler we had packed with shrimp, smoked pork, and manapua.

"Not too heavy?" my mother asked Caroline, who bumped the suitcase along the floor.

"Oh, no, it's fine," she said, setting it down.

"What inside the cooler?" Mom asked me.

"Just some things from Oahu. We better go put them in the freezer."

"No need bring nothing. Why you bring so much?"

"Not much," I said, carrying the cooler to the kitchen table. Mom followed behind Caroline, who was practically on my heels. "Just manapua, meat, and shrimp," I said.

"Shrimp?" she said, opening the cooler. "Shrimp expensive. Why you brought shrimp?"

"Only little bit," I said. "Here, we can help you put it inside the freezer."

We put away the freezer items, then returned to the table. "Why two dozen manapua?" she asked, opening the box. "One dozen enough."

"No," I said, teasing her. "I think you can eat one dozen by yourself."

She turned to Caroline. "No listen to what he says. That one knows how for tell stories."

Caroline laughed along with my mother, who stopped her

laughter short when she recognized it. "You like take bath?" my mother asked, changing the subject. "The water hot."

"A bath sounds lovely," said Caroline. "Spencer told me about your hot tub."

"Hot tub?" said Mom, confused. Her lips pursed at the idea of comparing her old tub to a modern apparatus on the cover of slick magazines. "We call it furo."

"I can't wait to try it," said Caroline.

We got our clothes and towels before I led her outside to the washhouse, where our family's bath area comprised one-fourth of the square building. "When I was small," I told Caroline, "the old people walked naked to their baths."

"What?" she said in disbelief.

"Not kidding. Maybe I was playing outside, and they walked by naked, or with one small towel."

"I thought Japanese were supposed to be modest," she said, looking around the inside of the washhouse.

"I don't know. Had old people that walked naked. Just like it was nothing."

"Look at that," she said, her head inclined. "The walls don't go all the way to the ceiling."

I laughed. "Gotta be careful what you say in here. You never know who going hear."

"But what about when you use the toilet?" she asked. "You mean everybody can listen to everybody else?"

"Before days, we did it on purpose," I said. "Taizo and

William would go in the other corners so we could all use toilet at same time. We'd shout 'bombs away.'"

"Oh, please," she said.

"Come. I can show you the furo tub." We stepped past the partition to the furo bath and pulled back the accordian-style cover. Caroline reached into the water with a finger.

"It's boiling," she said, pulling away the finger. "Who could possibly take a bath in there?"

I laughed, testing the water with my pointer finger. "Not me," I agreed. "Too hot for me."

"No kidding! Do your mom and dad actually take a bath in this water?" she asked.

"Everyday," I answered. "But they finished already, so we can add cold water."

We took the cover completely off the wooden tub so that steam could escape, and added cold water to the tub's brim. Then we washed ourselves over the drain in the floor, rinsing with a bucket of water from the furo, and took turns getting in and out of the wooden tub.

"Too hot," Caroline squealed after about twenty seconds, jumping from the tub.

"Here, let me try," I said. "I get the right kind blood." I made a great display about getting in, but lasted only half a minute or so before I leapt from the water.

"What happened to that blood of yours?" Caroline teased, drawing a line on my chest with her finger.

"Cannot help. Look, the wood still burning. The water getting more hot while we wait."

"If I get in that water again," said Caroline, "I'm going to pee."

"Then no get in. You going ruin it for me."

"For you?"

"Maybe later I like climb in."

"Don't forget to let me know so I can watch," said Caroline, drying off with a towel.

"You might be sleeping," I said.

"Wake me up," she insisted, pulling a shirt over her head. "I wouldn't want to miss it."

That night we slept in my childhood bed, awakening at four in the morning to the calls of chickens from Filipino Camp. I held Caroline, awake in my arms, and asked that she be patient with my family.

"Wait till you meet mine," she said, giggling.

We spent the morning on the roads and paths of Wainoa, walking in circles around the town and the mill. I led her to Taizo's gravestone, where she bent on one knee and pointed to the Japanese characters of my last name, now hers. Next door, at the Buddhist church, I taught her to take off her shoes before entering. We lit incense in the small room behind the altar. Caroline hugged me as I held my brother's urn.

We left the church, and I gave to her some of the gifts of Wainoa. In Chinese Camp I climbed a tree for two yellow guavas, then watched her lips pucker at the idea of eating the seeds. We walked to the beach, where I shimmied up a palm tree and knocked down a green coconut. Caroline clapped so proudly that I didn't show her until later how badly the rough bark had scratched my inner thighs. We split open the coconut and from each other's fingers ate the soft, spoon meat of the young fruit. She said it tasted like vanilla pudding.

We drove in the afternoon to Iao Valley, where I found ginger flowers and made whistles for us both. Next, Caroline swam in a hidden bend of the Iao stream while I told her of ancient Hawaiian battles in the hills around us that turned the stream blood red.

She sat on a rock to dry, huddling arms over legs against the tropical breeze, and I wished I had brought my camera. I liked how her hair lay flat against the back of her neck—the way it curved, then straightened. I have always liked water on my wife.

My mother had fixed a plentiful dinner by the time we returned. She took her place across the table from Caroline and me, nudging toward us the bowls and platters of food. My father, she apologized, had already finished eating. Since our arrival he had not spoken to us, but neither had he interrupted the growing acceptance by my mother, a compromise that I felt was difficult for him.

Before we left in our rental car for the airport on Sunday afternoon, my mother presented Caroline with a patchwork quilt. It was, she said, our wedding gift, a gift too large to mail. We brought it home in our suitcase, stuffing our clothes into the empty cooler. That very evening, Caroline replaced our store-bought comforter with my mother's quilt. We sat in bed, the quilt spread over our knees, and I pointed out the materials I recognized.

"Look, how obvious," I said, pointing at a square. "This my army fatigues."

"I prefer this quiet lavender color."

"I'm not sure where that came from. Maybe she bought it. But look this one over here," I said, lifting the blanket to isolate the square. "An old rice bag. Look, can see the writing."

"Oh, I can," agreed Caroline, fingering the blue and red lettering. "How long do you think she had that material?"

"Cannot guess," I said. "Could be years."

"How long do you think it took for your mother to make the quilt?"

"Long time," I said, pulling it to our shoulders.

"But we only got married a couple of weeks ago," she reminded me. "Could she have made the quilt that quickly?"

"No," I said. "Takes long time for her to make."

"Then do you think she knew?" asked Caroline. "Do you think she understood we were going to get married no matter what?"

Could she have? "Maybe," I said, thinking back to how she had pleaded with the lifted shoulders, the tightened lips, the strained eyes, for me to reconsider the marriage. She must have known, and her pain was sewn into the quilt now above us.

Teresa was only two weeks old when we first took her to Wainoa. My wife and I had been back many times in the four years since our marriage, and though my father had begun to verbally acknowledge Caroline, he had gone no further. Yet, when we brought Teresa to Wainoa, he walked over to my mother, who held the infant in cradled arms.

"Look the hair," my mother said to him. "Japanese hair."

"Haole skin," said my father.

"Get Spencer's eyes," Mom noted, stroking the baby's chin.

Dad extended two fingers and carefully touched the skin of Teresa's arm. Mom lifted the child toward him, and my father nodded. He accepted the baby into his arms while I held my breath, watching. Caroline's fingers pressed into my elbow.

"What the name again?" asked my father, looking into the eyes of his only grandchild.

"Teresa," said Caroline.

"Teresa Kikue," I added.

Dad nodded very slowly, his eyes intent on the child's. He rocked her, a man's solid sway. Finished, he walked over to Caroline and placed the baby in her arms, taking special care with the child's head. I think he must have touched my wife; it did not appear otherwise.

"Some pretty the hapa baby," my mother said, choosing the local word for a half-Caucasian child. "One day you going need chase away the boys."

"Take care her," Dad said to Caroline.

She answered, "We will," to my father's back as he turned and left the room.

That evening while we conversed with Mom in the parlor, Dad carried the futon bedding into the room. His arms stuck straight out so that the bedding lay flat upon them. Though I had never in my life seen him carry any type of linens, he appeared only slightly uncomfortable, like a man unused to carrying a handful of proteas. As far as I knew, the futon had not been taken down from the closet since my auntie had visited from Kona for my high school graduation.

"What that for?" asked Mom, looking up from her sewing. "Why you carry that?"

"The baby," my father said, nodding with his head toward the child, who lay in Caroline's arms. "Teresa need place for sleep." He knelt and with a curious gentleness lay the bedding at the foot of my mother's sacred altar. He spread it neatly, then went to Caroline. "I can carry?" he asked.

"Here," she said, lifting Teresa.

The transfer of the child was awkward between them, each reaching when the other wasn't quite ready, but finally Dad held Teresa. He settled her closely to his chest and carried her to the futon, where on two knees he lay her down.

That evening in bed, with Caroline's back nestled against my chest, I explained the history of my mother's sacred altar. "Was one wedding present from her parents," I began. "During the war, she needed to hide it in the closet."

In the next room, Teresa lay peacefully on the fine bedding my father had prepared for her. It was her habit to suck herself to sleep, and Caroline and I listened, hushed, as our baby sucked loudly the knuckles of her tiny hand, unaware of the honor given.

CONVERSATIONS

I have come for another weekend with my mother. She visibly weakens, now, between each of my visits. When she told me a few months ago that she was dying, I leaned forward onto her kitchen table. Since then, I have consciously straightened my body, but the leaning goes on within. I hold on where I can.

The toll for accepting her impending death has been cumulative. I go to bed each night, but sleep little, as my mind sifts the layers of the past in desperate excavation. Even as I dig, I'm scared to look.

We are talking in the parlor. I sit in the koa chair before realizing it is now too far away from the couch upon which she rests, as if the tiny parlor has suddenly grown more spacious. I note the surprise in her eyes, the lift of her chin, but she says nothing as I settle closely beside her on the couch.

She has not worn street clothes for my visit. Her bathrobe hangs loosely from her tiny, curled frame. I touch her ankle and rub my fingers upon her lower arm, where the bones push cruelly against her skin. Her muscles have begun to weaken, to fail, to disappear. A layer of my mother is disappearing.

Her weakness maddens me, twirls my gut. The anger shames me, and I try to control it. Methodically, I acknowledge what has become of a strong woman's body. Her shoulders hunch. A deep hollow arches her back. The upper body leans forward, head toward the feet. I look for yellow in the whites of her eyes, and discern perhaps a tint, but I'm not sure. I don't want to look too closely.

"Anyway," my mother says, "I notice you never bring me my pistachio nut this weekend."

"No," I say, setting her hand back upon her lap, "I only brought anthuriums and manapua. Never get time to go Vegas."

"Good, then," she says, smiling. "Caroline must be some happy. Can go shopping with the money you never lose."

"Try wait," I tell her. "I'm going to be rich one day. Watch for my picture in the California Hotel newsletter. Front page, big winner."

"Yeah, well, better hurry already. Pretty soon going be old and then money no mean nothing." She nods toward the altar. "Only people comes important at the end."

I follow her eyes to my father's picture. He stares toward me from the working years, the cane years. Time chiseled strongly

the lines of his face. Taizo carried that same strength of character that has nothing to do with muscle. Thinking of my
brother, my eyes pass to his picture.

We have come far during these months of my mother's illness. Taizo's eyes no longer avert mine. We have not yet begun
to speak, but I now listen cautiously for his voice. Our distance,
I know, is closing.

Wind carries the sound of the ocean through the screen door,
rattling it in its frame. As a young child, I recognized nothing
but potential in water. After Taizo's death, I became more aware
of the limitations. Water washed the life from my brother. His
death washed some of the life from my mother. I think of that
long-ago winter as waves of water that washed my family bare.

The phone rings on the table. I pick up the phone, still
ringing, and hand it to my mother. She answers and speaks
furtively. I sense that she is uncomfortable with my nearness and
walk to the kitchen. When I return down the hallway a few
minutes later, she says, "William came."

His name freezes me in position across the room. "When he
came?" I ask carefully.

She doesn't look at me. "Other day."

"You saw him already?" I ask.

"Did. He looks good. Going come tomorrow for see you."

I walk across the room and return the phone to the table.
"Why you never told me he came?" I say, sitting further down
the couch.

She shrugs. "Was going to."

"Where he staying?"

"Lahaina-side."

"Just like one tourist," I say. "Figures." I feel angry that she has welcomed William, who brings the past with him. "Mom?"

"What?"

"Who told him to come?"

"What," she says, "somebody have to tell him for come? Maybe I like see him."

I feel I must know, and say quietly, "You asked him to come?"

"Never mind," my mother says dismissively, so that I feel like a reprimanded child. "Only thing important is that William stay here."

"And brings all the bad memories with him," I say.

"Shouldn't," she says. "He never do nothing to you. Sometimes I think you blame him after Taizo die."

I suck in my breath. "What Taizo get to do with this?"

"You tell me."

"You like talk about Taizo?"

"I think you the one who need for talk. More better you stop blaming William."

"I'm not sure where to start."

"Just talk. The words going come."

My breathing pauses, held against words. I fear continuing this conversation. My heart senses a possible avalanche, a letting go. Except for my father's words behind the washhouse, the rain-soaked cry in my mother's throat as they pulled Taizo from the reservoir, my parents never questioned me about Taizo's death. They allowed William and me to handle the knowledge as if together we could bear it, could keep the horror contained in the realm of childhood. How could they have known that horror chases grown men?

"You never blame me," I begin, careful to look away from her. Without the face-to-face acknowledgment, I don't have to see the memory of Taizo in her eyes.

"No sense blame," she says. "Only boys."

"All the time I kept waiting for questions that never came."

"Your dad, that's why," she says.

The statement turns me toward her. "Dad?" I ask, puzzled.

"He said for leave you boys alone. One time Uncle getting ready for ask you and William, but Daddy came all mad."

My hands cradle each side of my head, near the ears. "I never knew," I say.

"He said you and William going get hard time already. No need make it more hard."

My lungs pause and then breathe in this surprising information. Dad knew the truth and had protected me from the others. Guilt seeps, circulates, as I accept that my father could feel compassion.

"Besides," my mother adds, "we knew."

"No can," I say. "Cannot."

"Can," she says, nodding. "Same like I stay there." She closes her eyes, thinking. I watch the lids, creased and folded, until they again open to the present. "You see," she continues, "in my mind he die over and over. My oldest boy die one hundred times, one thousand times. Every time I stay there."

We sit quietly, remembering, and lean our shoulders gently toward each other's, but we do not quite touch. William now sits between us. I try not to think about anything for a while. My mother must be thinking about changes, losses, because when she again speaks, she says, "The Yamada home gone."

"I know," I say. "I saw when I came."

"Pretty soon this home going be gone, too."

"That I don't like see. What's the plantation going do with all this land after the houses are gone?"

"I don't know. Make subdivision or something." She covers a yawn with her hand.

"You tired?" I ask.

"Little bit."

"Can go bed."

"I going soon," she says. "Humbug, you know. Every time I come tired."

"I can help you to bed," I offer. "We get plenty time tomorrow."

"No need help me." She pushes away from the couch and stands. "Tomorrow can go church?" she asks. "Can go early, before William comes."

"Sure," I say, happy at the idea of my mother changing from her bathrobe. "Can go anywhere you want."

I head for bed and lie on my back in the dark room. In that bed of my childhood, I begin to retrieve images of light breaking up the darkness of a New Year's Eve. Harder to recall is the unbounded sound of firecrackers, their reckless shatter. The old people of Chinese Camp said the fireworks chased away evil spirits, but for me the thrill was purely in the noise.

Every New Year's Eve except the year of the strike, we played with fireworks until midnight when my mother frantically waved us inside to change our clothes. She believed we needed to start every New Year clean, including our underwear. She began right after Christmas, cleaning windows, washing curtains, ordering us to cut our toenails, unsatisfied until the house and its family had been thoroughly scrubbed. No Fujii escaped my mother's annual cleaning.

I smile, remembering how relentless she could be, until an ugly feeling creeps upon me. I try to shake it away, but it clings to me, this idea that now my mother is dirty, and that, perhaps, she had no bath today.

The next morning, I awaken before my mother. From her open doorway I watch her sleep. My breath and shoulders stiffen as I regard her vulnerable body, the way her open mouth stretches toward air. I want to close her open mouth, slam it. A stubborn part of my mind still believes she is a healthy woman who should sleep after me, and awaken before.

Alone in the kitchen, I drink a scalding cup of instant coffee, then another. She hobbles into the kitchen as I begin my third cup. I insist that she sit down while I fix her coffee and a piece of toast that she can pretend to eat.

"What?" she says, nibbling at the edge of the toast, "not eating nothing?"

"No, only coffee."

"Can make for you," she offers, beginning to stand.

"No. I only like coffee in the morning."

She sits back down. "Suppose to eat breakfast."

"Never mind," I say. "I cannot eat this early."

"At least one piece toast. Everybody get room for one piece toast."

"No, thank you," I say. "Just coffee."

"I guess you stay old enough to know if you want breakfast."

"I guess I am," I say.

"Let me know if change mind."

I nod. "You ready for church?"

"Not yet," she says. "What, you like take me church in bathrobe? Not too polite, that."

"Why not?" I tease. "Maybe can give the old reverend one thrill."

"Terrible, you. What son would say that to his mother?"

"I cannot help. You made me like this."

"Crazy," she scoffs. "Nobody made you like this. Poor Daddy never know what for do about you."

"And only good I turned out," I say, daring her to continue.

"I don't know about that. The way you talk. Terrible, you."

"By the way," I say, "how come you never offered me any breakfast? I might like some toast."

"Listen to you! Terrible! Terrible, terrible, terrible." She mutters the word that best describes me. I wince in mock pain. We are secure in the pretending. My mother loves me through everything. Tenderness underscores her words. On and on she mutters, terrible, terrible, terrible. Somewhere in the long string of terribles, her voice cracks. Then her eyes water, I think. She hurries from the room before I can be certain.

Should walk or take car?" she asks as we step into our slippers and down the front steps.

"The car," I say. Does my mother actually believe I'd ask her to walk to the end of the block? "Might as well make use of the rental car."

"Can walk, if like."

"No, can take the car," I say. "Hard to believe we never had car in the old days."

"Never need," she says. "What for need car? Everything stay close by."

"True," I say, opening the passenger door and helping her inside the car, "but not everything was good back then."

"No. Old days was hard life. Maybe that's one good thing about coming old. No can remember bad times."

We drive to the church. She offers the red, heart-shaped

anthuriums to the gold altar and prays. Her sick, arched body reminds me of a woman in permanent bow. When she finishes with prayer, we open the door behind the altar and enter the room of ashes.

My father's ashes rest in this room. He speaks my name as I light a stick of incense. The voice calls softly, a tone of his later years, the black hair beginning to gray, the features beginning to soften. Incense burns its smell into the air, into my thoughts. My mind drifts on smoky thoughts, half-understood.

Then I accept once again, as I have so many times, that Taizo's ashes are also in this room, although I have never considered them at rest. Uncle Toshi, Auntie Sachi—they too are here. I think of how my mother will be next and the idea sickens me. I can't stay too long in this room.

My mother surely understands. She allows my arm to pull her to my side. I guide her from the church and we return home. There's no other rental car in sight as we pull into the driveway; I'm relieved that William hasn't yet arrived. As we step from our slippers to go through the front door, I notice my mother's slippers have been left side by side, ready to be easily stepped into at her next departure. In contrast, my own slippers lay haphazardly, one of them accidentally kicked a few feet across the porch. Although I have had a lifetime of practice, my slippers seldom align.

Inside, my mother settles on the couch with a patchwork blanket. I look past her, out the front window, watching for a rental car to come down the dirt road. I still don't feel ready to see William. "If I take one walk," I ask her, "you going be okay?"

She sighs, but then forces a smile. "Go on."

"I'll just be gone a little while."

"Go long as you like," she says, pushing away the blanket and standing. She walks me to the doorway. As I step into my slippers, she encourages me to go with a wave of her hand.

"You sure you going to be okay?" I call from the road in front of the house.

"Take long as you like," she answers, closing the door between us.

I turn from the home and begin to walk. It occurs to me that I haven't been back to our school since high-school graduation, when my shoulders were piled with congratulatory flower leis that I couldn't see past. It seems a good place to walk toward.

I head up the dirt road my father used to trudge from plantation to home but mostly, it had seemed, from home to the plantation. It was also the road to the store, to church, to year after year of school. My parents always knew that our little dirt road could take their children anywhere.

The sun shines heavily and tingles my skin. A University of Hawaii baseball cap keeps the sun from my eyes so that I can step carefully, avoiding the puddles from recent rains. I don't slow down until I reach the perimeter of the schoolyard, where four little girls play with fluorescent jump ropes. They look at me suspiciously, as if I don't belong here. I figure that I might know their parents, and I try unsuccessfully to figure out their ancestries. One looks at least part-Japanese, and I can discern some Filipino in the skin of another. Yet I can't determine their ancestries with any certainty.

I walk over to the narrow shade of a royal palm and touch the smooth trunk. My fingers search the bark for rough edges. I think of the many little hands, mostly brown, who have touched this tree. When I was a schoolboy, a person could neatly divide my classmates by ethnicity. This would no longer be possible with much accuracy. The bloods of Hawaii are mixing together.

I try to visualize the hands of my own daughters upon this trunk. The color brown carried forward in their skin, their eyes, but the lightened shade disguises their Oriental blood. Their eyes remember a trace of Japanese and also the Scandinavian of their mother's blood. There is blue behind the brown, the certainty of a larger world for my island-born children, a bloodline that has opened the arc of their eyes.

I push away from the tree and turn to study the school. The original stone building appears unchanged, like teachers who are old when you're in their classroom, and then look exactly the same decades later. What has changed is the schoolyard itself. I shake my head in disbelief as I realize what has become of the schoolyard. The grass has almost completely disappeared under rows of portable classrooms. It seems sad to me, because I was a boy who lay on the schoolyard grass until I itched.

I begin to wander back through the camps, noting the concrete slabs where houses used to be. But when I reach Supervisors Row, it is exactly as I have remembered.

In front of a particularly grand house I pause to study the oversized doorway, the same one an innocent boy so boldly walked through many years ago. The house and yard still appear spacious and well kept. The grass has been freshly mowed, and the pleasant smell reminds me of the times Tom and I rolled across it. I smile at the memory of his crinkly blue eyes.

With one foot propped against the decorative wooden fence, I think back to when Tom moved away in his junior year of high school. The night before his family left for the mainland he came over to say good-bye. My father called me out of my bedroom.

"Yes?" I asked, stepping from my room.

"Your friend came," my dad said.

I looked up to see that Tom stood just inside our front door. My father must have asked him in. Puzzled, I looked at Dad, and he nodded before leaving the room. I turned to face my friend.

"Came for say good-bye," said Tom, who now spoke the same as the rest of us.

"When you leaving?" I asked.

"Tomorrow."

I nodded slowly, then smiled. "Not fair, you know. This the second time you going over the ocean."

Tom laughed. "You going get your turn, Spencer."

I nodded, unsure what to say next. Tom stuck out his hand,

and I shook it. I was suprised when he reached around with his other arm and hugged me. I hugged him back, and then, with just a wave from my front walk, he was gone.

I shake away the memory and take one last look at the front entrance. As I turn from the house and begin walking away, I wonder where Tom lives now. Was his doorway ever again this big?

The rest of Supervisors Row means little to me. I wander down the road that cuts through Wainoa's cane fields. Mini cranes gather at one end of the field, searching for worms where plantation equipment has recently unearthed stalks of sugar. Here, where the sugar cane grows, I realize how deeply I still love this valley, though not all that has become of it. A short stretch down the road, toward Wailuku, a tourist business flaunts a huge orange-and-yellow windmill. I wish the plantation would surround it one night and set it on fire.

The cane fields end at the main road, which I cross. There, on the thin stretch of sand, I kick away my slippers. I step into the shallow edge of the Pacific and reach down to meet the water with my hands. Water flows over my wrists and ankles. It seeps into the sand, which now covers my toes.

I watch the approaching waves and imagine them as galloping horses making their way toward shore. The flow is steady. My mind pounds with the sound of hooves.

"Spencer."

I recognize William's voice. Slowly, I shake the water from my hands and turn around to face him.

"I thought I'd find you here."

I can feel the water washing against the backs of my legs as I study him. Time has handsomely aged my cousin. He stands with his hands in his pockets, pants legs rolled up, and I recognize my father in his face. Yet William's eyes are simple, looking at me in quiet anticipation.

"Why you came?" I ask.

"I heard your mother was ill."

"She has cancer," I say.

He nods.

"She was happy you came," I tell him.

William folds his arms, watching me. I walk past him and sit beneath a leaning palm. My hips settle between two roots, like one child's legs around another. I feel him eyeing me, and when I look at him, he does not turn away. I am not surprised.

Neither of us speaks for a while. Finally, I speak of the ocean. "Only Hookipa get more colors of blue."

"Blue is blue," he says, picking up a rock and tossing it into the ocean.

"No, cannot be," I challenge from beneath the tree. "Cannot be only simple."

"Maybe not," he concedes, sticking his hands in his pockets. "Maybe it's not quite that simple."

My eyes strain to see the depths of his. "She's dying," I say.

He nods. "I heard."

"William?"

"What is it?" he asks.

"Maybe this will be our last chance to talk about when Taizo died."

"What is there to talk about?" he asks, as if it's something he's never considered.

"We never talk about what happened."

"You're the one who didn't allow me to say anything." He reaches down for another rock and throws it far out into the water. He sits down with his hands wrapped around his legs. Without looking toward me he says, "You might not like what I've got to say."

"Anything is more better than silence."

"Maybe not," he says, staring out at the ocean.

I sense he is warning me, but ignore the warning. "Talk to me, William. I need to hear whatever you like say."

He lay down, his back upon the sand. "The others died a natural death," he says.

"What?" I ask, wishing he would sit up and face me.

"Your dad, my mom and dad. Their deaths were natural. Taizo's wasn't."

"Taizo's death was natural," I say, puzzled.

"Accidental is not natural."

"Was," I say. "Was one natural death."

"Call it what you want. It was practically murder."

"Murder? You can call Taizo's death one murder? Not me. We only were children."

"I've had all these years to think about it," William says.

I push up from the roots and walk over to stand above him. "If his death was one murder, then who killed him? Was me? You? Who then? Tell me who," I demand. I reach down and grab his arm.

He sits up and yanks his arm free. "That's what I haven't yet decided."

"Oh, no. No tell me that. You mathematicians always get answers. Everything stay solvable, right? So no go telling me you no get the answer."

He sneers, angering me further. "There's an answer," he says. "I simply haven't found it yet."

"After all these years? Wrong, you. Taizo died one natural death. No say nothing else."

He stands, brushing the sand from the back of his pants. "Don't pretend, Spencer."

"Who pretending?" I ask, arms wide.

"You. Your whole world is pretend. In fact, it always was."

"Sometimes never get one answer. Can search all you like but never going find. You know why? Not even there. Why you think get the color gray?"

In a condescending tone he says, "Don't go philosophical on me."

"Okay, never mind then. Only stop looking for answers." I gesture wildly, out of control. "We were little boys inside cane fields. If need to blame something, blame the sky. Blame the sun for coming so hot that day. Blame the cane, William, blame the cane. Only, no go blaming us. Not you and me. Nobody loved Taizo more."

"Why did he do it?" William asks. He speaks quietly; his cheeks relax.

"You mean Taizo?" I ask, slumping upon the sand.

"Why?" he repeats, bending down next to me on one knee. "Why do you think he did it?"

"Had to," I say. "Taizo never get choice."

"He was only a young boy himself," William says. "I didn't realize that until I grew much older."

"Not like us. He was never like us," I say, bending my knees and resting my head against them. "My mom says that when Taizo was born, she wanted him to have one English name. My dad said no. The oldest boy cannot forget tradition."

"Taizo didn't need to be reminded," William says. He stands, looking down on me. As I look up at him, his hand stretches toward mine and pulls. "Let's go together to see your mom," he says.

I nod, thinking of how she will smile to see us enter the house together. "We go."

He playfully taps my arm. "I don't remember talking as strangely as you."

"Don't tell me you forgot pidgin English."

He shakes his head. "I doubt that I forgot anything."

We cross the main road and walk until we are surrounded by

fields of cane. "You know," I tell him, pausing to look at the cane on all sides, "one day this cane all going be gone."

He nods, his eyes scanning the rows. "I drove past Waiehu and saw the macadamia fields."

"The sugar companies need to do something. Only losing money. Plenty people like stop them from burning the cane. Every time get letters in the paper about the smoke."

"I can't imagine Maui without sugar cane," he says.

"Get ready," I tell him, though I feel unprepared myself. "One day when you come visit, the sugar will be gone."

He nods tentatively, and we continue walking. William leaves the road, touches some cane, and returns in a loose diagonal to my side. It's hard to believe so much time has passed since we walked this road together just before my high school graduation.

William flashes an evil grin at me just before he jumps into a puddle of water and splashes mud on my legs. I find my own puddle and dirty his pants. We run about that road like we are carefree little boys again, protected by the privacy of tall sugar cane.

After a time we settle into our ages and walk like mature men, but that's boring. I find a stone and kick it to William. He returns the stone with a perfect shot. I feel like hugging him, but instead I line up the stone with my slipper and concentrate on my aim.

COMPANIONS

walk with my companion cane. Tired, worn, my body leans upon the morning winds.

Morning winds . . . mourning winds. Last night the phone rang. I knew instantly why it rattled me from sleep, and I ran for the phone, reaching for the receiver with the certainty of a lit match against dry cane. Then, hand on the receiver, I let the phone ring one more time. Knowing she was going to die had not prepared me for the blood waves that shook my body cold. I want one more day with Mom.

My forehead pressed, pressed, a rhythmic pressing, as I flew here on the day's first flight. I have returned to Maui, the island of my birth. The plantation boy wants to be alone with his cane.

One hand shades my eyes as I look past the cane to the sugar mill, where the chimney stacks blow smoke, then turn in the opposite direction to glimpse the quiet ocean. Both the mill and the ocean bother me, pulling my eyes and thoughts into the distance. I walk to the edge of the cane road and sit in the dirt. My legs draw close to my body and I wrap my arms around them. Now the cane is my horizon, all that I can see. The peaceful cane begins to soothe me; my breathing slows.

A baby centipede crawls upside down along the edge of a cane leaf. A spider as big as my hand crosses my ankle. I recognize a sudden urge to kill them, to watch the spider collapse into a stilted ball, legs bent and folded, to watch the centipede splat. With my hand I raise my slipper above the spider, catching it in shadow, then simply watch it scuttle away to sunlight. I turn now to the centipede, knocking it with my slipper from the leaf, but can bring myself to do nothing more than startle it. After a brief recovery, it waddles back to the cane, alive.

My mother once told me about losing her way in the woods above her home. In the old days there were camps in the mountains. There, my mother lived. She was about ten years old when she wandered away. After a time of realizing she was lost, she found her way again near the forbidden water flume that cut through the mountains and sent harvested cane to the mill. She said she watched the cane floating past and imagined herself doing the same. She lay on the ground and hung her head over the water flume. She thought she saw some colors in the water, blues, reds, sparkles of yellow, and she maneuvered so close that the bottom of her hair sipped water. As she watched, the colors disappeared, and she imagined them also floating downward toward the mill where some worker would discover them. But then her parents were suddenly behind her, grabbing her hands, one parent to each side, and their calloused palms led the way home. She was fine, she was safe, and yet her parents mourned the near loss. They shook their heads and looked at each other. They walked too quickly and pulled my mother's arms at the shoulders.

The parents escaped the loss of their daughter and instead, one lifetime later, I mourn the death of my mother. She was the last member of my family to live in Wainoa. We must have been weak. Even the cane has managed a stronger survival.

Death connects. In one death I think of another and, for me, all deaths go back to Taizo. I have come to these rows of protective cane because in my mother's death, my brother has again begun speaking to me.

Taizo is the only one of us whose voice never aged, who remains a solemn-faced little boy when I bring his face back into focus, and all because of a day when good boys had to be bad. I am sorry for that day. The bad boy grew up to become a sorry man.

I lay my chin upon my knees and purposely glaze my eyes to see him. The focus is honest, immediate. Taizo wears denim overalls on this last day of his life. He stands patiently while William and I aim our guava-branch slingshots at a flock of mynahs. Our stones wobble, fall short. Taizo aims toward a seemingly empty tree and downs two birds, sparse pigeons, with his Red Ryder BB gun. I watch with envy as he etches two notches on the gun's wooden handle. We cook the birds over a fire and eat them for lunch. Taizo smothers the fire with handfuls of dirt that stream from the tilted sides of his cupped hands.

We climb a huge monkeypod and play tree master, jumping with boyhood carelessness from branch to branch in a game that my mother could never bear to watch. After, we find a spider web and toss beetles against it. The spider wraps them like sacrificial mummies.

We sit in a circle, the kind of circle that young bodies often draw. We are boys with our backs to the world. Two of us are brothers; three might have been.

"Now what can do?" I ask, fiddling with my slingshot. "Would be good day for go swimming."

"Junk, swimming," says Taizo, who can't even swim.

"But would feel good," I say. "You can watch."

Taizo rubs dirt against the length of his gun. "What else can do?"

I lay my slingshot down in the dirt beside me. "I like swim in the reservoir."

"No even talk like that," says Taizo, looking with one eye into the end of his gun. "Not allowed."

I speak carefully, watching Taizo with each word. "Nobody going know."

He eyes me and lays the gun in his lap. I look at William. He grins, nodding eagerly. "I not going tell."

"Danger, that," Taizo says, erasing William's grin. "All mud on the sides. Hard for come out again."

I speak sarcastically. "Not danger. William and I know how for swim."

He ignores the sarcasm. "Is too danger. Why you think not allowed for go?"

"I going," I say, chin up.

William pats me on the arm, getting my attention. "I like go, too."

I nod my approval to William. "You coming?" I ask Taizo.

He won't answer. He won't even look at me.

"Never mind," I tell William. "Him only grumble." I stand and pull William up to my side. Together we walk toward the reservoir, a stream dammed by the plantation to catch water for the cane. I figure Taizo watches us walk away. I don't turn around to check, just in case I'm right, and I make sure William does the same.

Stripped to our underwear, we peer over the edge of the reservoir. The water begins about six feet down. Slimy remnants of plants smear the muddy banks.

"You ever went inside before?" William asks.

"No."

"How we get down there?"

I study the water, considering. "Need for slide down the mud."

He steps back from the edge and crosses his arms. "Scared," he admits.

"Not," I say, trying to dismiss his fear. "Going be good fun, like one slide."

His face and shoulders cringe. "Still scared."

"I can go first," I assure him. "You watch and do same like me."

Sitting, I push over the edge and slide feet first down the slippery mud. As my feet hit the water, I remember that some boys at school claim it's fifty feet deep. Whatever the depth, I sense that my feet aren't anywhere near the bottom and quickly swim back up to the surface. There, I raise my hands toward William, who watches me from above.

"Come," I encourage, treading water. "I going catch you."

He shakes his head. "Too scared."

"No be scared. Not going be like Taizo, are you?"

He sits down and edges forward gingerly, his little legs over the side. "I like watch for little while," he tries.

"Now," I say, beginning to get angry. "Now or never."

He rocks in a motion of indecision, then pushes over the edge. His feet slide toward me. My eyes close against the spattering mud. William lands in my arms, and we go under.

"Good fun," he says when we come up for air. "Can slide again?"

"No," I tell him. "Just swim, and then we need for get out."

We float on our backs. My tongue tastes light raindrops that fall into my open mouth. Through a blur of light rain, I see Taizo bending over the edge above me. "Get out," he demands. "Rain coming."

"Not going to," I say. "No need listen."

"Good fun," adds William, floating on his back.

Taizo thrusts both arms in the air. "Starting for rain. Get out."

"No can make us," I say. "We not scared like you."

Taizo folds his arms and hugs his body. I sense that he is genuinely afraid. Behind him, the sky has darkened. I tread water and speak quietly to William, not wanting Taizo to think he has any influence on me. "We better go," I say. "The sky coming dark."

"Not scared of rain," says William.

From above, Taizo yells, "What if rain hard? The water going come fast. You stay in one stream. Now get out. Get out!" As he shouts, the sky bursts into rain. Taizo continues shouting, but I can no longer understand him. His words are blurred.

William clutches at me, his arms tight on my neck. I peel away his hands and heave him toward the near bank. "Climb," I order. "Time for get out." I follow him to the bank and begin climbing.

Mud oozes through my fingers, even as I try to grab hold of the bank. The bank pulls away from itself, pieces dropping into the water. My feet slip on the slime of mud and plants. I reach desperately, wildly, hugging the mud with the length of my body.

From somewhere, Taizo calls my name. I think I hear William crying. Yes, my little cousin cries. He calls my name in repetitive whimpers. Oh Lord, William cries.

I close out his voice, but I do not act quickly enough against the voice of my brother. Taizo screams. I hear my brother's screams as I lose hold of the bank and fall back into the water.

The fear closes in on me like a cat from behind. I cannot shake loose that panic, that cat. Like the water that is everywhere, the cat closes in on me, scratching to get in, and hisses at my ears, that insidious hiss at my ears, until my fear becomes total and the cat is me. On cat claws I climb the mud of the reservoir to safety.

Only then do I remember that William still fights the water. I watch from above as the back of his head goes under and his mouth reaches toward air. His young face is splashed with mud. In horror I realize his lucky ears, filling with water, have betrayed him. I lie down and reach my arm over the side toward William.

Taizo touches me on the back of my shoulder, a gentle touch of long ago. That touch pivots my face up toward him, a look at the side of his face. His feet pass by my face as he jumps into the water. The water splashes against his body. My mouth opens in silent scream.

All these years later as I sit in the cane and remember that childhood day, my body curls in shame. I had coaxed William into the water, then left him to get out on his own. I watched as Taizo helped William from the water, allowing him to climb his body as if a ladder. William stepped on the top of Taizo's head. He climbed free and lay down on his stomach, spitting mud. I was running to my father for help, my mouth yet open in silent scream, when Taizo died.

Now, four decades later, I hear my brother's voice. He has not forgotten our childhood fields of cane. They were everywhere. We thought sugar cane covered all the world's valleys.

Taizo calls my name without distance, without anger. Although I am grateful for the lack of anger, I value more the lack of distance. Distance, I have learned, caused my greatest pain.

My brother and I are together again. Unacknowledged years lurch inside me. I want to fill in the silence of my long-ago scream at the reservoir, sensing it is all I need to forever close the empty years between us.

And so, with the cane as my buffer and Taizo as my companion, I scream through the leaves and the rows and the fields. I am the wind among cane stalks, weakening as I make my way inward. I fear the scream will resolutely pierce my soul, too painful to bear, but then I hear my brother's voice. The scream soothes, looking for rest, the pain as weary as two young brothers late to bed, calming, gentle, warm, and a peaceful Maui green.

MY

LITTLE

BROTHER'S

CRADLE

The sugar plantation prepares cane for its own death by turning off the irrigation water. Without water, the cane's supple dance in the Maui wind collapses into a death rattle of drying green. Outermost leaves fall to the dirt. Insects suck the cane's veins and roots. Finally, when field workers set the weakened cane afire, the plant hasn't enough life to fight the flames.

How many cane fires have I watched in my lifetime? I cannot begin to count. As a child I watched the cane grow its way toward death. Wainoa fields were incrementally planted, and on a day's wandering, I could study cane in all of its stages. I never felt much emotion toward the young plants and preferred the cane long and lithe. I remember standing along the edge of growing cane and Taizo stepping back, analyzing, and determining that a particular field of cane was now taller than I was. Only from that point on did I take a sincere interest in the field. I was accustomed, I suppose, to looking up at everything upon which I depended.

Later I would walk past one of these mature fields and recognize from its raspy death call in the wind that it was scheduled to burn. With my eyes open, heart guarded, I came to recognize the symptoms. From my bedroom window, when I should have been sleeping, I could watch the orange fires against the black night sky. That was important for me. I wanted to see the fires, the funerals.

The ashes flew on the wind throughout Wainoa, and we called them "Maui Snow." When I unknowingly slept through a cane fire instead of watching from my window, I was horrified to happen later upon the charred aftermath, a field of ashes. I found myself stumbling unprepared upon a graveyard and realizing I'd missed the funeral.

With the same horrid sureness that I have learned to recognize, death came for my mother. My mother. Death's approach didn't fool me. It was as if someone had turned off the water.

My mother didn't fear her own death. That, I believe, was her farewell gift to me.

Last Sunday, during our final afternoon together, she was unable to leave her bed. She lay on her back with an IV tube attached to one hand. I lifted the tubing and sat carefully alongside her hips. "Can hear the rain?" I asked her.

"Can," she said.

I was taken aback by the apparent effort in the breathy voice. "No need talk," I said. "Just listen."

She smiled, continuing as if I hadn't been alarmed. "You like rain," she said to me. In her voice, I heard the raspy sound of wind through dying cane. I winced at the recognition, thinking that silence could somehow keep my mother alive. Yet she wanted to speak, she clearly had not finished with words, and I leaned nearer her to better hear. "Good, the rain," she said.

"Yes," I told her, smoothing the pillow, feeling her breath upon the back of my hand. Her elbows pushed against the bed as she repositioned her head on the pillow.

"Not comfortable?" I asked her. "Not comfortable, your pillow?"

"Comfortable."

"Can get you something?"

"No need."

"Let me know. . . ."

She nodded. "You know that picture with the slippers?" she asked.

"I kept it all these years," I admitted, "even if you told me to throw it away."

"I like it," she said. "I just never wanted for tell anybody."

"You like it?" I asked.

"Yes. Just no tell anybody, but." She grinned at the conspiracy between us and, confident that her secret would remain safe, she closed her eyes.

"The nurse coming back in one hour," I said to her closed eyes. "Then I need to go."

"No worry."

"Next week the whole family coming. You care for anything special from Oahu?"

"No, nothing."

"I cannot get any more time off work or I would stay."

"I going be fine." Her eyes struggled open. "Son?"

The whites of her eyes were yellow, absolutely. I looked away from them. "What is it?" I asked, focusing instead on the triangular pattern of her blanket.

"Turn this way. All the way. I like look at you."

I didn't immediately respond. The blanket was many-colored, and the triangles were patched into circles.

"Spencer?" she asked.

I lifted my face and looked at her.

"There," she said. "I wanted for look."

"No good you look at me," I teased, unable to speak any more death talk. "Only old, me."

"You?" she said, following my lead. Her voice lightened, elevated. "Some young, you."

"Then how come every time Teresa and Amber say how old I am?"

One corner of her mouth smiled. "All your gray hair, that's why."

"Hey, you. Black, this hair. Never mind little bit gray hair."

"At least get hair," she said. "Better not complain."

"Anyway," I said, "what do kids know? They think anybody with gray hair is old already."

Her eyes again closed, and our light talk closed with them. Her breaths crackled in her throat.

"Why not come stay with Caroline and me?" I asked her. "How easy would be for us to take care of you. This way we only worry."

"No need worry," she said behind closed eyes.

"What if get pain? Maybe you not even going say nothing if get too much pain."

"Pain nothing for talk about," she said. She pushed up to her elbows. The strength was temporary, and she lay her head back onto the pillow. The blanket had slipped, and I rearranged it so that it covered her chest. "Spencer?" she asked.

"What?"

"Take the altar."

"I will."

"Today."

"Next time. No worry. Next time can take."

"Take already. Mrs. Sato got the box for you."

"Next weekend can take. Can wait till then."

"No. Today."

I did not want to take the altar. My head shook at my mother's closed eyes. My throat caught the pain that I didn't want her to hear. Carefully, forcefully, I shoved the pain back down to silence.

I knew what she was doing. She was leading me where she thought I needed to go, leading the son toward the mother's death. She had sensed a lingering reluctance.

"Okay," I said to her. "I can take the altar."

She smiled. "Now. Go pack already."

"Oh," I teased. "Some demanding, you."

"Better hurry then."

While she lay in her bed, I packed her altar. As I wrapped the framed photos of Dad and Taizo, I supposed my mother was listening from her bed, hearing the crackle of the newspaper that would protect them from her home to mine. The altar had been hers since her wedding day. As I lowered it into the box, I wondered about what my mother had prayed and whether solace had been granted her. I thought she must feel a deep loss in knowing she would never again stand before her altar, but when I finished with the packing and returned to her room, her cracked lips were smiling.

"Took everything?" she asked as I knelt at her bed.

"Did."

"Everything?"

"Yes. Only thing left is the matches."

I heard the front door open and close. The nurse's voice called from the parlor, and I knew I had to be getting to the airport. Thoughts of Caroline and the children helped to comfort me. I fleetingly wondered if Amber would meet me at the airport in her hula costume, an outfit she favored above all others. I teased her about constantly wearing it, though I liked how the material brought out the gold in her skin.

Reluctantly, I let go of my child's image and sat back down on my mother's bed. "Almost time to go," I said to her. She rolled to her side and curled her body around my hips. "The nurse came," I said.

"I heard."

We didn't have anything else to say and sat quietly for a few minutes. I stood over her, then, and kissed my mother's forehead.

"Good-bye, Mom. I need to go now."

"'Bye, son. No need worry."

"We're coming next weekend. Tell the nurse to call if need anything."

"No worry," she told me again.

At the doorway I paused for another look at her. She watched me from her bed as if I were a framed picture on her altar. I had seen her look at Dad and Taizo in the same way.

"Good-bye, Mom."

"No worry, now."

"I not going worry," I lied.

I drove away then from Wainoa and from Mom. I left her in death's reach with the hope it would carry her away gently, the way she had long ago carried William from one row to another.

Wainoa was closing in on me. As I drove past the fields of

green, Maui green, I mourned cane's possible disappearance. Gone would be the all-encompassing fields of my Hawaiian childhood, the sugar cane that enveloped and sustained and enticed little boys into its fields. Instead there would remain only the unforgotten days, when sugar swayed as softly as my little brother's cradle.